NOX

LORDS OF OTHERWORLD
BOOK THREE

STELLA RAINBOW

Contents

Dedicated to:
Every reader who gave the men of Otherworld a chance.

ONE

Nox

Okay, so this hadn't been my smartest decision. In my defense, I was tired of not having any answers, of having to scrape up any little piece of information we could find, only to discover it still didn't help one bit.

I knew entering the Chasm without telling anyone had been a stupid thing to do, but if I'd told anyone, they wouldn't have let me come, and we needed answers.

The problem was I hadn't realized my staff wouldn't travel with me. If I'd taken a few moments to think about it, I'd have realized that the magic of the realms wouldn't let a weapon that could help the black souls escape come anywhere inside the Burning Chasm. After Artemus and I had reinforced the tower with our combined magic, the only way a black soul could go in or out was through my staff. Of course the magic didn't want it anywhere near the black souls.

But that meant that I was now effectively stuck in the Chasm until someone came to my rescue. Considering I'd taken pains to make sure no one saw me entering the Chasm, they probably didn't even know I was gone. How long would it take until someone noticed? And would they even be able to figure out a way to get me out?

Ugh, okay. That was enough panicking. There was nothing I could do to get myself out of here. I'd need to leave that up to my friends. Instead, I needed to focus on why I'd come here in the first place.

I needed to gather intel. I needed to find out exactly what was going on in the human realm and here, and I needed to do it before I was spotted by any of the black souls.

I looked down at myself and sighed at the blob of white I saw. Well, I wasn't a literal blob, more like a slightly human-shaped puff of white smoke. I tried to lift my hand, and some smoke drifted off my side. Great. Just great. Now I didn't even have a body to manipulate.

I'd been in this state very briefly when I'd first died in the human realm, and then a soul collector had come and picked me up, and I'd regained my body once I came to Otherworld. And now, here I was, back in my soul form in a place full of black souls, where I'd stand out like a beacon.

I tried to walk forward, and my smoky body zipped forward at an alarming speed, smacking against the wall of the tower.

"Fuck," I groaned, then startled as I realized I could speak. Thank the fucking Afterworld. With my current luck, I wouldn't have been surprised if the Chasm had its own language that only the black souls understood. Fuck, it could still happen.

Plus, there was the little fact that I still hadn't entered the actual Chasm. I was still hovering in the tower aboveground, the entrance to the Chasm a few feet in front of me. It was nothing fancy, just a hole in the ground that seemed to emit enough heat that I was seriously worried about damaging my beautiful skin by going closer.

Well luckily, you don't have *any skin*, a voice in my head that sounded an awful lot like my friend Zane said.

I rolled my figurative eyes at it before inching closer to the hole. Unfortunately, it wasn't the kind of hole I wanted to be inching closer to.

I didn't smack into any walls this time, but the heat was unbearable the closer I got to the entrance. I wanted to stay right here and wait to get rescued, but I couldn't do that. I'd come here for a reason, and I needed to complete my job.

If the worst happened, I was hoping I'd "die" and move to Afterworld, and then it would just be a matter of Damien visiting me so I could give him all the information I'd have hopefully collected by then.

Was I ready to leave Otherworld and spend a peace-filled life in Afterworld? No. But I'd still do it to save my friends, and that was that.

I thought of all the people I wanted to protect from the evil that was brewing in the Chasm. Walker, a child who found this realm of the dead a happier place than he had the human realm. Damien, who finally had his mates after years of pining. Zane and Wren, who'd just found each other. All my other friends in Otherworld who were more than friends to me. They were my family.

And so, to protect the family I'd left behind, I steeled myself and jumped.

The heat as I floated down was unbearable. It got hotter the lower I went, and I realized there were levels. Different levels with different intensity of heat. I hadn't realized that. I'd assumed every soul sent into the Chasm suffered the same exact fate, but it seemed like the magic had different plans.

I was tempted to stick to one of the top levels, but I knew the information I needed wouldn't be there. The people responsible for everything from the supe murders to the child kidnappings weren't the kind of people the Chasm would go easy on. To find them—and the infamous queen of Underworld—I'd need to get to the bottom of this. Literally.

The challenge would be keeping myself hidden. Experimentally, I tried curling up to see how small I could get without losing my sight. I gasped when I realized I'd turned into a palm-sized sphere, the same shape souls went in when they were being carried by soul collectors. I'd assumed only soul collectors could make souls take that shape, but I guessed a soul could do it themself if they wanted to. I reverted back to the larger form for the moment, deciding I'd make myself smaller when I needed to hide since it was harder to manipulate the smaller form.

I jerked back when a flame licked at my soul, surprised when I didn't feel anything but the utter hotness of the flame. Experimentally, I shifted closer and gasped when the flame touched me but didn't burn.

Could the flames only hurt the black souls? Thank fuck for small mercies.

While the heat was awful, I could deal with it. And since the flames didn't burn, I could use them as a hiding place if I needed to.

I eyed the rest of the Chasm beneath me, a dark hole that I couldn't see more than a few feet of despite the fact that it was all flaming.

Taking a deep—figurative—breath, I steeled myself and took the plunge.

Harlan

If someone had told me I'd one day die all of a sudden protecting the people I loved, then wake up in a different realm and watch my mate—who I'd *just* seen for the very first time, and that too only from the back—walk into what sounded like a suicide mission, I'd have thought they were high. Or under the thrall of an incubus. Or just plain crazy.

But that was what had happened, and I was having a hard time catching up. It didn't help that a passing glance in a mirror had shown me a reflection that I hadn't seen for decades. My hair didn't have gray in it anymore; my skin didn't have any wrinkles. I looked like I was in my twenties by human standards. The man I'd first met when I'd woken up had told me it was part of being an Otherworlder, but I didn't understand why. What was the point of looking younger?

I was deflecting, and I knew that. I was thinking about all this stupid shit that didn't matter because I didn't want to think about the real problem: my mate had run headfirst into a suicide mission, and it looked like there was nothing I could do to help him.

"When I get my hands on him, I'm going to take back his cloak and all the clothes I gifted him with. That'll teach him." I blinked at the man I'd been told was the king of this realm. He definitely *looked* like a king. He was over seven feet of muscles, with wicked-looking black horns sticking out of his head, a tail that snapped like a whip from side to side, and midnight wings that were folded against his back. He looked like the devil, but his words were anything but.

"For that to happen, we'll need to get him back first," Zane, the person who'd been showing me around when we'd seen Nox leave, said.

"We will find him, Zane. I promise you that. He used his staff to get through, didn't he?" Damien asked as he picked said staff off the table. A whole bunch of people were crowded into this meeting room, and I knew the only reason I was here was because I was Nox's mate. Everyone had been nice to me, but no one had wanted to waste much time over the hellos, and I was totally onboard with that, which meant I still didn't know the names of everyone here.

"He did. But unfortunately, I don't think any of us can use it. It's his tool, and only he knows how to wield it properly," a buff, warrior-like guy said, and someone snickered.

"Caelan," the king admonished, and a man with cat ears sticking out of his head—real, not the kinky kind—mumbled an apology.

"You're right, Maximus. The staff won't be able to help us, which means we need an alternate solution. We have to go with the assumption that Nox intended to use the staff to get back, that he didn't realize the staff would be left behind. Which means he has no means of getting out of there."

My heart stuttered in my chest, and I squeezed my hands into fists. Before I'd spotted Nox, Zane had told me all the gory details of the Chasm. Of how it was full of evil souls. Evil souls Nox himself had dumped into the Chasm. It was basically a pit full of the worst of humanity who shared a common enemy: Nox. And now Nox had basically offered himself up on a silver platter. Was I really mated to such a dumbass? I'd done some questionable shit in my lifetime, but this was in a different stratosphere altogether.

"So, how do we get him out?" one of the two women in the room, a dark-skinned, dark-haired lady with a voluptuous body and a calming aura, said.

"Could you get inside? I mean, you're the king, Day. Shouldn't you be able to?"

I wondered how the man who'd asked the question looked like he was in his forties when no one else here did, but it wasn't a question I could or should ask right now.

"He can't," a different man answered. This guy had long, golden-brown hair and a slim, model-like build. His green eyes shone as he looked between the two men, and I realized they were mates. The king and those two men were mates. "Damien is the king, yes. But the Burning Chasm is controlled by the magic of the realms, and only it decides who gets to go in. If it doesn't allow Day to go in, he won't be able to."

"What about King Tharion? Wasn't he supposed to come today anyway? Maybe he could help." A woman with blue eyes and blond hair spoke, her eyes flicking from King Damien to the man who'd spoken.

Damien shook his head, a frown marring his face. "I heard from Tharion this morning. Something came up in After-world, so he won't be able to come just yet. He said he'd be here as soon as he can, but we can't wait for him. I can try going into the Chasm. Maybe the magic will let me go. I don't think it'd want Nox to get hurt," Damien said, and there were murmurs of agreement.

"All right, that's one thing we can try. But we should think of an alternative if that doesn't work," the man with the cat ears—Caelan?—said, and I had to agree with him. It was always better to have a Plan B.

Zane leaned closer to the man beside them, who seemed to be whispering in their ear. Their eyes widened at whatever the man had said, and they shot him a look, to which the man gave a nervous smile and a nod.

"Wren suggested a portal. He hasn't tried to make one here yet, but he says he can still feel his magic when he focuses, so he's sure he'll be able to make it, but he doesn't know if he'll be able to make one that goes into the Chasm."

"Would a simple portal spell work if the king's magic doesn't?" I asked, speaking up for the first time.

Zane and Wren shared a look before Zane gave me a smile that was more of a baring of teeth—and their wicked-looking fangs—as they said, "Wren is an... expert at portal spells. If anyone can do it, it's him."

I sensed a story there, but again, this wasn't the time. So I merely nodded as Damien slapped his palms on the table and leaned forward.

"All right, everyone. Let's get our Keeper back."

TWO

Nox

Whatever I'd been expecting, this wasn't it. This place should have been chock full of black souls; it should have been teeming with them. And yet the area was strangely empty.

I eyed the entrance to the next level on the ground in front of me, not wanting to go deeper but knowing I'd have to if there was no one on this level.

Why were they so deep anyway? It got hotter the lower you went, so shouldn't they all be crowding in the top levels if that was what they wanted to do?

Gah, I really didn't want this mission to be futile. Damien would kill me if I died here without finding anything useful. Fuck. Fuck. Fuckity. Fuck.

Okay, okay. What would Zane do?

They'd probably go down knives blazing and find out everything they needed to know without losing a sweat.

Well, I had no knives. I didn't have their crazy bravado—just an unhealthy amount of impulsiveness and disregard for orders, apparently.

At least I couldn't sweat, huh? That was a plus point, right?

Ugh. I went to shake my head at my stupidity before realizing I couldn't because I didn't have a head now. I was just a ball of white smoke that could see. How did that work, anyway? Why were my senses working when I didn't actually have any ears or eyes?

The magic of the realms was weird sometimes.

The deeper I'd gone into the Chasm, the less human-like my body had become. It must have been the magic of the Chasm repressing my form. I didn't know how to feel about the fact that the Chasm was treating me—its very esteemed keeper—the same way it treated the dark souls that resided here.

Okay, enough dallying, Nox. Let's do this, I told myself, and then continued to stare at the dark hole for another few minutes before finally leaping in.

I jumped into the flames as I heard voices closing in, taking care to hide all of myself in the fire as they drew closer. They didn't have faces, obviously, so I tried to remember their voices so I'd be able to recognize them later if needed.

"It won't be long now," a nasal voice said, their smoky body glowing orange at the edges as the flames licked at them. For some reason, the flames didn't seem to be hurting them at all.

"Yeah, the queen is almost back to her old self," the other one said, his voice deeper and on the husky side.

"I cannot wait to show those Otherworld assholes their place. Especially that keeper who put us here." I narrowed my eyes at Nasal Dude, wishing I knew what he looked like so I could have the last word when I inevitably took care of him again.

"I don't give a fuck about them. I just want to go back to the human realm. There are no pretty boys in here."

I grimaced at the husky man's words, my insides churning at the thought of filth like this escaping back into the human realm. Damn, what was this queen planning? What would she even do if she got to the human realm? It wasn't like she could interact with anything or anyone there.

Right?

I needed more information, goddamnit. And since these two gossip guys seemed to be my best bet right now, I decided to follow them.

I had to stick to the flames, since everything else here was dark, and I'd stand out like a sore thumb. Thank fuck the flames didn't hurt me. Small mercies, eh?

I was surprised when the two souls reached another entrance to the level below and jumped in without stopping, without hesitating. *Why* were they heading even deeper?

There was only one way to find out. I gave them a minute so they wouldn't spot me the moment I came down and then jumped in.

The air was definitely hotter on this level, sweltering in its heat, and the flames larger, but the two souls scurried on as if they were unaffected. What kind of black magic was this? Wait. Was it really black magic? Had Jezebeth and Cynthia and all those other supes somehow brought black magic into the Chasm?

Fear rushed through me, and I tamped it down, refusing to let it freak me out. Not when I knew my odds were flimsy at best.

Hell, I couldn't even be sure if my friends were looking for me yet, let alone if they'd be able to find a way in to rescue me.

I was on my own for now, and I needed to make the most of my time here.

I stayed hidden in the flames as I followed the two dark souls down a dark hallway. I was starting to realize the Underworld Artemus had talked about had never truly been destroyed. The magic had just closed it off, added the flames, and renamed it the Burning Chasm. Because I was sure we were in a castle right now, and despite the dark walls and the fallen-apart decor, I could imagine this had been a grand palace once upon a time.

Every corridor we passed through had sconces on the walls with lamps that hadn't been burned in a long time. Bits of the floor that weren't covered in ash or flames revealed marble, and the stone walls seemed as imposing as the ones in the Brume Villa. While the villa was warm and welcoming, this place was sweltering and uninviting. It was hell in the truest sense of the word.

While I didn't feel the least bit sympathetic for the queen, I could imagine how someone who'd already been corrupted by the dark souls would do something like this when her "kingdom" was taken away from her. She was still batshit crazy, though.

Another level? I groaned internally when the souls leaped deeper into the Chasm. Again, I waited a minute before leaping in, my senses going haywire as the heat rushed around me, the jump feeling like it lasted hours and ended in a moment all at once. I aimed for the flames that were sure to be there, angling my ball-shaped body toward the edge of the corridor.

Except there were no flames. The level I ended up on was devoid of fire and ash, and as I'd suspected, I shone like a beacon in the darkness.

The souls I'd been following whirled around to face me, and they gave a shout when they spotted me. Before I could react, or escape back upward, I was surrounded. And I meant literally surrounded on every side by gross, sticky dark souls.

"The queen will be happy to see you, soul collector," the nasal-voiced man said. Oh, maybe they hadn't realized who I was. That could be helpful.

"I don't think he's just any soul collector. Are you, Keeper?" the husky-voiced one said, and I groaned loudly. I was caught already, so what was the point of staying quiet?

"Come on, the queen is waiting," he commanded, and then the dark souls were carrying me through the hallway.

Queen of Underworld, here I come.

Harlan

"We need to hurry," I mumbled under my breath, hating the fact that there wasn't much I could do. At least, not until the king had tried his way first. Not that I wanted him to fail, of course.

"Reece, is your shield ready?" King Damien asked, eyeing the older of his mates. Reece gave him a firm nod, and he turned back to the Chasm, stepping forward and placing his palm on the tower wall.

"Artemus, come here, please. You helped Nox secure the tower. It might recognize you," King Damien said, and his other mate hurried forward, placing his own palm beside the king's much larger one.

I could see the glow of magic that arched out of their hands, but I could also see the tower fighting it off. It didn't want to let them in. They didn't belong inside. And yet it had let Nox inside. Why? Had the close proximity to the Chasm affected Nox more than everyone here seemed to believe?

"It's fighting back, the tower. It won't let me enter," Damien growled, and Maximus, who'd been standing behind him, jumped to the side as his tail smacked him in the thigh.

I paced a few feet behind the others, eyeing the tower as I tried to keep myself from panicking.

I hadn't even seen Nox yet, not his face at least. All I'd caught a glimpse of was his brown hair and the oversized cloak he'd been wearing, the cloak that was now draped over Zane's arm, Nox's staff in their hand. I had half a mind to go there and demand they give them to me since *I* was Nox's mate and therefore should be the one to take care of his things. But it was clear Zane was a good friend of Nox's, and I didn't want my first impression to them be that of an asshole.

I didn't know what kind of man Nox was, but I knew he was my mate. I also knew he'd happily risk his life to protect his friends, and the fact that I was here was enough to show that so would I. I'd chosen to stay in Otherworld for the sole reason that I'd be able to check up on my sister, my niece and nephew, and my best friend, even if I couldn't ever actually talk to them.

So yeah, even though I'd never talked to Nox and didn't know him at all, I knew enough about him to be worried about what he'd do in there. Vaishnavi, the dark-skinned, dark-haired chief from the meeting, had explained to me that if Nox were to "die" in there, he'd simply move on to Afterworld. He wouldn't be gone forever.

But the fact was I didn't want to move to Afterworld. I wanted to stay here, where I'd have the ability to check in on my family. Where I could be a part of the Anubis squad and destroy people like Cynthia before they hurt more innocents. I didn't want to move to some heavenesque realm where I could lay on the beach and sip martinis all day. That wasn't the kind of man I was, and I didn't know who I'd pick if the choice was between my family and my mate. I'd rather not have to make a choice at all, which meant I needed to get Nox out of there. Soon.

"Goddamn it!" Damien growled, punching the tower in his frustration. A crack appeared on the wall, but after a moment, it wove itself back, as if the tower was determined to not let anyone in through its walls.

"We'll figure something out, sweetheart," Artemus murmured, placing a palm on Damien's shoulder.

"He's in there, Arty. Alone. Probably scared even if he wouldn't admit it to himself. His staff got left behind. He knows he can't get out on his own."

"His staff!" I gasped, snapping my fingers. Turning to Damien, I explained, "You said Artemus and Nox secured the tower together, right? What if you try to channel Nox's magic through the staff? Maybe the tower would recognize it?"

Damien's eyes widened, and Artemus hurried over to Zane, who handed him the staff. "It's worth a try," Artemus said as he returned to Damien's side and handed him the staff.

Damien curled his fingers tight around the staff, pressing the gem against the tower wall as Artemus placed his hand beside it. The gem glowed brightly as the two worked their magic in tandem, and I watched as their magic enveloped the shield around the tower, cajoling it into letting them in.

The protective magic sparked once, twice, before it blazed brighter, physically pushing Damien and Artemus back a few steps.

Zane rushed forward and jerked the staff out of Damien's hand a moment before he swung his arm in a move that would have snapped the staff against the tower and probably broken it in two.

"Calm down, you jerk. Nox will be mad if he returns to find his staff broken. Again," Zane snapped, and my brows shot up. Had they just called their king a jerk?

Damien rubbed his palms over his face before glancing at Zane, his golden eyes flashing. "You're right, sorry. We need to get him out of there, Zane."

"And we will. It's time for Plan B," Zane said, their eyes turning to their mate, who looked like he was about to puke. I didn't know what his story was, but I knew he was the only one who hadn't said a word since I showed up here. At least not out loud, though I thought I saw him whispering to Zane a few times.

"We need to try the portal," Damien agreed, not sounding the least bit happy about it. I knew he didn't want to endanger anyone else by sending them into the Chasm, which was why he'd been so resistant about the portal idea, but hell if I'd let anyone else go in there to get him.

Nox was my mate, and I was going to rescue him if it was the last thing I did.

THREE

Nox

The queen was a more defined blob of black than the rest of her "subjects," and surprise, surprise, she had glowing white eyes, as if being the queen of the world's vilest beings wasn't creepy enough.

"Ah, Keeper, it's good to see you. I've heard a lot about you from my people," the queen said in a voice that seemed to echo in the dark, cave-like structure they'd brought me to. It didn't look like it was part of the castle. Had they dug under it? Was that how they'd avoided the flames? But how did they have the energy to do that when the Chasm supposedly made them so weak they couldn't even have a physical form?

My eyes strained to catch more details of the place we were in, and I realized the queen was hovering over a throne-like structure. Had her minions salvaged it from the castle above? All for the sake of posturing? After all, it wasn't like she could actually sit on the throne.

"Can't say I feel the same," I said, trying and failing to shift around. The dark souls were stuck to me like glue, the fucking bastards. "Frankly speaking, I didn't even know you existed until a few days ago. You must be very forgettable."

The queen's eyes flashed red before turning white, and when she spoke again, her voice was deceptively soft. "I imagine you're here to find out what my grand plan is, hmm? Since I have no plans of letting you go, I'll let you in on them. It's the least I can do to make up for what I'm about to do to you, don't you think?"

Oh fucking perfect. The Queen of Underworld was a raging bitch. No surprise there. I'd only spent a few centuries outside the Chasm, and I still felt its effects on my psyche sometimes. This woman spent fuck knew how many centuries *inside* it. No wonder she was a bit... *extreme*.

"Oooh, is this the villain's monologue part?" I asked, hoping she'd keep talking. I wanted to know her plans, and I had to get her to tell me before she did whatever she planned to do to me. But I also had trouble keeping my tongue in check. It was an illness, really.

"Luckily for you, it is. I know you're mocking me, but once you hear my plan, you'll see there is only one way this ends: with me on the throne of Otherworld, and my souls back in the human realm where they belong."

Oh fuck, fuck, fuck. She wanted to get the souls back to the human realm? Had she lost every last scrap of sense she had?

"Even if they got to the human realm, it's not like they could do anything. Souls can't interact with anything in the human realm, remember?" The soul collectors were the exception, of course, but there was no way the magic would give the black souls that power.

"Oh, don't you worry, Keeper. I already have a solution for that. Haven't you wondered why my witches stole magic from all those supes who were too afraid to revel in what they were?

Or why that pack of shifters you fought had imbibed the blood of those supes?"

I held my breath as I waited for her to continue. This was it. This was what I'd come here for. The information that would make everything clearer, that would help us figure out what we needed to do next.

"The shifters were trials. Some of them had even succeeded, but your soul collectors had to stick their noses in. It wasn't a problem, though, because once the potion was ready, all we needed were a few supes no one would notice the disappearance of."

For the record, I did not like where this was going. At all.

The queen didn't need any encouragement to keep talking, which told me her minions didn't have much in the brains department, and she was probably starved for some intelligent company. Given my recent actions, I wasn't sure I counted.

"My loyal witches crafted the potion from some ancient texts, a potion that would turn the body of a person living in the human realm into a host for whatever soul claimed it first. It's a binding, unbreakable spell. As soon as my souls escape here, they'll have bodies waiting for them in the human realm. The supes are going about their lives with no idea that their days are numbered. Isn't that funny?"

"Hilarious," I deadpanned as my mind raced. This was bad. This was really, really bad. We hadn't even realized the living had already been involved. "There are way too many dark souls, though. You can't possibly have enough supes for them all."

"Of course not. I'll be sending five of my best to the human realm so they can turn more and more supes—and humans, of course—to our cause. Meanwhile, my other souls will help me reclaim my throne in Otherworld, and then I might dethrone the King of Afterworld if it strikes my fancy. Tell me, is Tharion still the king?"

Oh fuck. I needed an out, like right the fuck now. I had to tell the others all of this somehow. Soon.

I eyed the queen, something about the way she'd asked about Tharion piquing my interest. "Oh, Tharion's still the king. He and his mate rule it together."

Her white eyes blazed, and she let out a weird growl-scream-what-the-fuck. "Enough chitchat. Take him to the flames, people. Show him what we've suffered through while he sat in his cozy little house up there."

I loosened up at her command, shaking off the fear that had crawled up my spine. Didn't she know the flames wouldn't affect me?

I let the souls drag me with them as they led me back up to the last level where the flames still blazed, and they dragged me into the fire. I didn't fight them, knowing the flames wouldn't hurt me.

At first, it felt just like before, warm but not painful. Then I felt pinpricks of pain and realized I was burning, but only in the places where a black soul was touching me. What the fuck?

Before I could think anything else, the black souls pressed onto me, their black, smoky form mixing with my white one until it wasn't clear where I ended and they began. And apparently, the flames couldn't tell either because they licked at me like I was just another black soul, and fuck, did it hurt!

I tried to hold in my scream as long as I could, not wanting to give these assholes the satisfaction, but the pain was too much. A loud shout escaped me as I felt myself burning. I didn't have a body, but it felt like all of me was on fire. Everything from my hair to my toes.

Distantly, I wondered what I'd look like in my human form now. Ugh, I hoped my hair was okay.

A scream ripped out of me as a flame licked particularly deep, and I hoped my friends would get here soon because it didn't look like a quick "death" was anywhere in my future.

Harlan

"Um, Wren?" I asked, keeping a few feet between us because I'd observed Wren was a little skittish around everyone but his mate.

He still startled as he looked up at me, his blue eyes wide. After a beat, he swallowed and nodded.

"I know you don't know me very well, but Nox is my mate, and I need your help getting him back. Please." I'd sensed he was hesitant about creating the portal we needed, and I needed him to understand how important this was.

His eyes narrowed, the previous hesitance disappearing from his face as he pulled his phone out. I watched as he typed something on it, his movement jerky, before brandishing it at me. I leaned back since the phone was right in my face and read what he'd written.

He might be your mate, but Nox is my best friend. I would never not help him. I hesitated because of my own shit, not because I don't want to help Nox. I'll do the spell, and I'll get you in. But if you don't bring Nox back...

After a solid argument that lasted all of five minutes before a slim, fox-eared man ended it by reminding Damien and Zane that they'd want to go if it was their mate in danger too, they'd relented and given me permission to go find Nox, especially since I already knew how to use portals and manipulate them by adding my own magic to them if needed.

But as far as threats went, Wren's unfinished sentence was a pretty good one. I mean, the man was mated to the scariest person in the realm—and that was saying something when it was ruled by a man who literally looked like the devil.

"I'm sorry for doubting you. I'm just a little all over the place," I apologized, running my fingers through my hair in frustration.

Wren's face softened, and he patted my shoulder, giving me a small smile.

"Everything okay here?" I jerked back as Zane appeared seemingly out of nowhere, their eyes switching from their mate to me.

Wren took their hand in his and gave it a squeeze, and I stepped away, leaving them to it.

I paced in a circle as I watched Reece build a shield around the tower. Damien had declared we couldn't risk any stray dark souls getting out through the portal, and then Reece had suggested building a shield around the Chasm so anyone who escaped wouldn't be able to go too far. It meant waiting a little longer to get Nox, but it would also keep everyone else safe, so it was a compromise that needed to be made. Especially when the king's son waited in the villa with Caelan, who was apparently the king's best friend, though I also sensed a story there.

"All right, the shield is up!" Reece shouted, and I hurried to Wren's side. He met my eyes and gave a nod before stepping away from Zane.

Wren's fingers trembled as he raised his hands and started mouthing the words. He relaxed slightly when Zane pressed a palm to the side of his neck, and I wondered what his story was. Why was he afraid of using his magic?

Wren's hands fell to his side after a minute, and he shook his head, his eyes seeking Zane's.

Artemus had said the tower was resisting their magic, and I guessed it'd resisted Wren's too. What if...

"Wren! Can you modify the spell so you're not trying to portal into the tower but to the spot where Nox is? I mean, Artemus said the tower's resisting magic, right? But the Chasm itself is underground, isn't it?"

Damien eyed the tower before nodding. "That's right. The Chasm is all underground. Can you modify the spell like that, Wren?"

Wren took a deep breath and then nodded. He leaned toward Zane, and they offered him their ear. They nodded, before looking up. "Wren needs the staff. Channeling Nox's magic will be the easiest way to get the portal to reach him."

I'd taken hold of Nox's staff after Zane had grabbed it from Damien, and now I offered it to Wren. Mentally, I crossed my fingers and hoped this would work. Because if it didn't, we had no Plan C, and I didn't want to think about what that would mean.

Wren nodded and curled his fingers tighter around the staff before raising his free hand and starting the spell again. This time, I felt the magic stir around us, the feeling much stronger than it'd been before.

I held my breath as the magic grew stronger and stronger, and there. A little spot of white in the air. I watched as it grew larger, and I could see more colors. Red, orange, black.

And then everything disappeared as a scream pierced the air. I'd never heard Nox's voice before, and yet I knew it was him.

Without a second thought, I threw up a shield around me, a spell that was second nature to me by now, and jumped through the portal.

The heat was instant, but it slid off me as I rushed toward my mate. I still couldn't see him, since he didn't have a physical form in here, and if I looked down, I was sure I'd realize neither did I. He was surrounded by black souls, and it looked like they were holding him in the flames so it'd burn him. The fire licked at the dark souls too, but they didn't seem to be as affected. Maybe they were used to the pain by now?

As I reached him, I extended my shield to include him, and the black souls lost their grip on him, rushing away from me. I latched on to him before hurrying back the way I'd come, carrying him out of the portal with me.

All of it couldn't have taken more than a minute or two, but it felt like an eternity as I fell to my knees in the grass right outside the portal, my mate's unmoving body in my arms.

"Reece!" someone shouted, but all I could see was my mate's burned body. The upper half of his head seemed to have escaped damage, but the lower half of his face was badly burned, and so was the rest of his body. He wasn't moving. And I was afraid to touch him because I imagined it'd hurt. It wasn't like I could look for a pulse to make sure he was okay, anyway.

Someone kneeled beside me in the grass, their palm hovering over Nox's still form as I felt their magic stir, but I couldn't spare them a glance. All my focus was on Nox, on the fact that he still hadn't moved.

He needed to wake up. *Oh, please. Please don't let me have failed him. Please.*

FOUR

Nox

I groaned as I came to. Or at least I tried to. I didn't think I'd actually made a sound. My whole body felt like I'd just gotten the most wicked sunburn of my life. My skin felt hot and itchy, and I couldn't seem to move at all. Where the fuck was I anyway?

Right, the Chasm.

But wait. I'd been captured, hadn't I? And then... the queen had talked. A lot. Then...

I shuddered as I remembered the fire and the pain that had enveloped me when the dark souls had crushed themselves to me. The flames had hurt like a bitch.

But I wasn't burning anymore. So where the fuck was I?

My throat was dry as a desert, which was another thing that didn't make sense. I was a soul collector. I shouldn't feel thirsty. Fuck, I shouldn't feel so much pain either. What was wrong with me?

I made a weird, croaking sound and heard movement close by. I stilled, waiting for whoever it was to make a move. I was completely defenseless right now, and I fucking hated it.

"Nox! You're awake." It wasn't a voice I recognized, but the concern in the warm cadence of the voice was clear.

I moved my lips but couldn't quite make a sound, and I felt him shift closer. "You must be thirsty. Let me get some water."

There was silence for a few moments while I searched my mind for what had happened, and then I remembered.

A portal. A portal had opened in the middle of the fucking Chasm, and someone had come to rescue me. They'd carried me out, and that was the last thing I remembered. I didn't even know what they looked like, since they'd turned into their soul form too, but I was willing to bet it was the same person who'd just been at my bedside. Who was he, and why was he so concerned about me?

I opened my eyes, feeling better than I had when I'd first woken up. I still couldn't quite move, but the raging headache I'd had seemed to have quieted a little. Was that my soul collector magic working to heal me?

Eyeing the room, I realized I was in my cabin, in my own bedroom. The familiar surroundings had me relaxing into the mattress, and I glanced at the door as it opened and Zane walked in with a man I'd never seen before but recognized instantly.

He was the soul who'd come to my rescue. And now that I was seeing him without the flames, the dark souls, and with much less pain, I knew exactly who he was. My mate.

Holy fuck, he was my mate!

And what a wild first impression I'd made, jumping into the Chasm with no backup plan. Hell, I hadn't had a plan at all.

"Morning, asshole," Zane snapped as they walked closer to me, and my mate's brows shot up as he hurried after them.

I rolled my eyes at Zane, knowing their language better than most people in Otherworld. Zane was sweet to exactly one person: Wren. With Wren, Zane was a fucking marshmallow, but with the rest of us, they were a prickly porcupine. I knew them well enough to see the concern behind their harsh words, though, so I took a breath and croaked out, "'Lo, dickhead. Miss me?"

Zane narrowed their eyes and leaned closer, their fangs peeking out as they growled, "Once you're all healed up, I'm going to beat the crap out of you. And then I'm going to do it again, and even your white knight over there won't be able to stop me."

And with that lovely get-well-soon wish, they were gone. I hoped they encountered Wren before coming across anyone else because only their mate would be able to calm them down.

I blinked as a straw appeared in my line of sight and realized my mate—whose name I still didn't know—was holding out a glass of water for me. I gingerly wrapped my lips around the straw and took a sip of the cool water as I finally took the time to observe my mate. He was... well, he was fucking gorgeous. He had short, dark hair, gorgeous blue eyes, and his skin was a beautiful tan color. He was also built like a fucking tank, and if I could move, I'd climb him like a tree.

As I watched him, his eyes roamed over me, and I wondered what he was seeing. I hadn't taken a look at myself yet, but the clues—the pain, the inability to move, and how freaked Zane had been—told me I didn't look my prettiest at the moment.

I'd been so jealous when first Damien, then Maximus, and then Zane had found their mates, and I'd wondered if I would ever find mine. And now that I had, I wished he hadn't found me just yet. I wished he hadn't found me at what had to be the lowest point of my second life. Or probably all my lives.

"I'm Harlan," he finally said just as the straw made a hollow sucking sound and I realized I'd drained the whole glass. My throat thanked me for all the nourishment, and I whispered my mate's name, feeling a weird flutter in my belly as I did.

"Harlan."

He smiled faintly, though his brows were creased in worry. "Reece healed you, but he couldn't do it all in one go. You were too badly hurt. He said he'll be back once he's had a chance to recharge."

Considering it still hurt everywhere and I couldn't move a muscle, I didn't want to imagine how much worse it had been. It hadn't been long since Reece had healed a knife wound in my gut with just a touch of his palm, so I knew it wasn't his power that was lacking. If it weren't for Reece, I'd probably be in Afterworld by now.

Fuck, that was a scary thought. I did not want to have to deal with Tharion every day. The king of Afterworld was the least king-like king I'd ever come across, and that included Damien, which was saying something.

"You came for me, didn't you? In the Chasm?" I asked, my voice rough. It scraped against my throat as I spoke, and I had to swallow hard halfway through my question, but I got the words out.

"I did. Wren made the portal, though. He's quite powerful."

My brows shot up at that, and I winced as the stretching of my skin had pain lancing through it. Realization sank in a moment later, and my eyes widened in horror as I realized my face had been damaged too. Damn it, not my face! I liked my face, damn it. Fuck fuck fuck.

I dragged myself to the conversation at hand as my thoughts filled with a litany of curses and remembered what Harlan had said. Wren had done the portal spell to save me? He'd told me more about his past over the course of our friendship, and I knew what the portal spell meant to him, what it reminded him of. And yet he'd used it for me? I made a note to give him a big hug for saving me when I was healed and glanced up at Harlan, who was just watching me as if worried I'd take off to Afterworld at any moment.

"I'm okay, you know," I said, and he raised a disbelieving brow at me.

"Uh-huh, sure you are. I don't know you yet, Nox, but from what I've heard from your family, I have a feeling the Keeper of the Chasm might need a keeper himself."

It was my turn to raise a brow as a chuckle slipped past my lips, and I asked, "Oh yeah? And are you willing to take on the job, my knight?"

Harlan leaned closer, and I sighed softly as his fingers brushed over my hair, the only safe spot on me to touch, apparently. "I think I'm exactly the right man for the job, actually."

I blinked up at him, stunned for a moment by the brilliant blueness of his eyes. He had this possessive, warm vibe going that I really liked, and I wished I wasn't a crisp potato so I could throw myself at him like I so wanted to.

Holy fuck, was I burned down there?

I concentrated on trying to figure it out without giving myself away and realized that while my ass had definitely suffered some damage, my soldier and my jewels had been spared. *Phew.*

"Are you done with your assessment?" Harlan asked with a smirk, and my eyes widened as my cheeks heated up. Fuck, he'd caught me.

"Shut up," I grumbled, prompting him to laugh. He had a nice laugh too, warm and the kind that made you want to laugh along.

I smiled to myself as I returned my gaze to him. I might not have made the best first impression, but I knew Fate had a reason for everything, including the timing of when they'd sent Harlan to me. Now if I could just get back the function of my limbs...

Harlan

Nox definitely needed a keeper because he had no sense of self-awareness at all. His whole body had been baked over a fire, and yet I walked into the room ten minutes after he'd woken up—I'd stepped out to tell the others that he was stable and didn't seem to be in too much pain, though I had a feeling he was hiding the worst of it—to find him trying to get out of bed.

"What the hell are you doing?" I demanded as I rushed to his side, my hands fluttering over his shoulder as I tried to stop him without actually touching his hurt skin. After Reece was sure Nox was stable, he'd focused on numbing all the major pain points and drying out the skin so it would hurt less, or something to that effect, but I didn't want to worsen his condition by touching his damaged skin.

"I was bored," he said, and I stared at him, aghast.

"Wasn't your earlier adventure enough excitement for the day?"

He gave me a sheepish smile before sinking back into bed. "Why don't you tell me about yourself? You know, so I don't get bored again."

I rolled my eyes at him but settled into the armchair I'd dragged closer to his bed earlier. I liked his place. It was rustic and warm and homey, and it kind of reminded me of the cabin I'd lived in for the last months of my human life.

"Well, you know my name. I'm a warlock, or I was in the human realm. Zane said supes don't stay the same when they come to Otherworld, though their mate seems to still have his magic, so who knows."

"How did you die?" Nox asked, and it was such a weird question that I had to laugh. It didn't feel real, to be honest. I felt like I'd portaled somewhere new, not that I'd died and been reborn—sort of—in a different realm.

"Well, a witch was trying to kill my best friend and his mate, and I was trying to protect them," I explained succinctly, and his eyes widened.

"You're truly a knight, huh? And you're talking about Cynthia, aren't you? I'm glad that bitch finally got what she deserved," Nox said, his gray eyes flashing at the end.

"So I gather she's dead?" I asked as relief coursed through me. With everything that had happened since I'd woken up, I'd forgotten to ask anyone about what had happened to my friends. Guilt washed through me at the fact that I'd forgotten about them so easily, but I shook it off.

"Oh yes, Maximus and Lionel took care of her. Don't worry."

"Holy fuck," I mumbled as I realized something.

"What? What is it?"

"I just realized that it was Maximus who'd brought the kids to Mistvale, to our clan. I'd tried to figure out what he was when he'd shown up, and I hadn't been able to. No one in the human realm knows about Otherworld, right?"

"Some do. Maximus's informants, and I think some of the older supes suspect the human realm isn't the only realm. But for the most part, no. No one knows about the other realms."

I shook my head as I recalibrated everything I'd known in the human realm with everything I knew now. When I hadn't said a word for a few minutes, Nox started twitching again, so I focused on him again. He was like a little kid hopped up on sugar.

"So, why did you go into the Chasm? I got the sense that something big was happening, but no one has filled me in yet," I asked, not only because I wanted to keep him busy until Reece returned, but also because I really wanted to know. I needed to know what the danger was and where it would come from so that I could keep Nox safe.

"It's a long, clichéd story, to be honest, but here's what went down: A few centuries ago, we had another realm called Underworld. It was where the black souls were tortured for their crimes by demons, and the forgotten queen ruled over it." Nox shifted around, turning on his side so he was facing me. I was halfway up, ready to help, but he waved me off, and I resumed my seat, waiting for him to get comfortable.

"So anyway, after a while, the magic of the realms realized that the black souls poisoned everything around them and that no amount of punishment would make them better. So the realm was turned into the Chasm. The queen was too poisoned by then, and couldn't leave her realm as a result. People pretty much forgot about Underworld and its queen for the most part, and life went on."

I handed Nox a glass of water when his voice started going out, and he drained it completely, returning it to me as he smacked his lips and gave me a grateful smile.

"Fast forward to the present, centuries of peace later, a few years earlier we found a witch who'd been draining rare supes of their blood—and thereby their magic. We thought she was working alone, but now we know the queen of Underworld somehow contacted her and other witches like her in the human realm and made them do her bidding. She intends to claim the throne of Otherworld and free all the black souls, and the whole 'I'll rule the world' thing most villains claim they'll do."

I blinked at Nox as he finished speaking, so stunned by his deadpan delivery that it took me a few minutes to process everything he'd said.

"And where did the kids come in? The ones Maximus brought to Mistvale?"

Nox frowned and then winced as his burned skin was stretched. I slid my fingers into his hair again, petting him softly since that seemed to be the only way I could touch him without causing pain.

"They'd been kidnapped. Apparently, magic refilled faster in kids, so they were being held and regularly drained of their blood."

Fuck. Raiden—the dragon who unofficially headed the Mistvale clan—had implied the kids had been abused, that they needed gentle care, but this wasn't what I'd imagined it to mean.

"Well, I'm glad Maximus saved them," I murmured, thinking of my little niece and nephew and what I'd have done if someone had hurt them.

"Me too. We're going to stop them, Harlan. Once and for all."

"We are. But for that, you need to get better first, yeah?"

Nox rolled his eyes and blew out a sigh. "I know. And I know it was stupid, going into the Chasm alone without telling anyone. I was just so frustrated. We had no leads, and these people are just out there hurting innocents. I needed to do something. We needed information, and I knew I was the only one who could get it."

"You might've been the only one who could get it, but you didn't have to do it alone. If you'd talked to the others, made a plan, you could've had Wren waiting to get you out once you were done," I said, hating that he'd had to suffer so much pain before I got to him. If only I'd been a little quicker.

"I know that!" Nox snapped, before his eyes shot to mine. "Sorry, sorry. You're right. I see that now. I shouldn't have gone off alone. I should've trusted my friends, my family. They had my back even when I'd intentionally left them out of my plans, and that tells me just how big of an idiot I was. I have a lot of apologizing to do," he ended wryly, and I smiled.

"That you do. Zane might be at the top of the list, but Damien and Artemus are a close second, I think," I said, and Nox winced again.

"Oof, that is not going to be fun."

"Knock knock, did someone order some common sense?" a voice called, before the bedroom door opened and Damien stepped into the room. He had to stoop low to pass through the doorway, and I bit back a smile at the image.

"Ha ha, you totally cracked me up, your highness," Nox drawled, and I shook my head in awe. It hadn't taken me long to realize that while Damien held the title of the king, none of the other soul collectors treated him any differently. He was one of them, and that was definitely something special.

"Oh, if you think that was funny, just wait until I tell you you'll be taking a leave for the next four weeks. I don't want you anywhere near the frigging tower."

"Well, seeing as how your mate left me half-healed here, I don't think I'll be moving anytime soon," Nox sassed, and Damien's eyes lit up, mischief clear in them as he hovered over Nox.

"Oh, that's a great idea. Maybe I'll just tell Reece to hold off on healing you completely. Maybe then you'll do what you're told for once in your life," Damien said, but I could tell it was an empty threat by the smile he was trying to bite back.

"Oh fuck, no! Have you seen this guy?" Nox demanded, his eyes flicking to me before turning back to Damien. "You are not going to stop me from climbing him like a tree."

I could feel my cheeks turning red, and I glared at Nox, to which he merely winked back at me. Lord, he was going to be quite a handful, wasn't he?

FIVE

Nox

"...And that's when her monologue ended, and then she had her minions carry me off to be crisped. The fire hadn't hurt me before, but when the dark souls clung to me, it fucking burned." I shuddered just thinking about the pain. It was much better now, but I could remember every moment of the burning like the memory had been branded into my brain.

"The first thing we need to do is find those five supes," Damien decided, and I had to agree. The Chasm was as secure as we could make it, but like we'd just seen, there were ways to get in and out, so we had to ensure the dark souls wouldn't be able to claw their way into the human realm.

"You're right. How will we do that, though? It's not like we know anything about these supes."

Damien grimaced, his tail swishing in his agitation. "That's true. We'll figure something out. I'm heading to Afterworld in a bit to update Tharion about everything. It sounded like he has some history with this queen. If he knew her before, there's a possibility he might be able to help us in some way."

"I wanna come," I whined, and Damien raised a brow at me.

"Come on, then. I'm not stopping you," he challenged, and I narrowed my eyes before heaving myself into a sitting position. Except I didn't. I merely strained a few inches off the mattress, my body unwilling to move beyond it.

"Harlan, you can come in now!" Damien called, and I glared at him as Harlan stepped back into the room and immediately hurried to my side.

"What are you doing? Lay back!" he growled in this commanding voice that I obeyed without thought.

Damien grinned widely, a knowing look in his eyes as he fluttered his fingers at me and left the room.

"You really have no sense of self preservation, do you?" Harlan shook his head before resuming his seat, his dark hair standing up on ends.

"I'm not used to doing nothing, that's all. I don't know how to just lie here," I grumbled, and his expression softened.

"I get that. I truly do. I hated staying still when I was in the human realm. There was always something I needed to do, you know? But you also have to understand that if you try to do what you want right now, you'll only create more problems, and not just for yourself. If you hurt yourself more, it'll take Reece longer to heal you. And if you take longer to heal, you won't be able to help the others, and they'll worry about you instead of focusing their all on this problem. You see where I'm going with this?"

"I do, I do. I'll try not to be as difficult. You know, I was so jealous when all my friends started finding their mates, and I would wish every day that I'd find mine soon. And now that I have, I've made an utter fool of myself in front of you since the moment you first saw me." I glanced away from him as I spoke. I wasn't usually shy or unable to look someone in their eyes, but I felt weirdly vulnerable right now. And stupid.

"You didn't make a fool of yourself, Nox. Sure, you made a bad decision, but that's not all I saw. You know what I thought when I found out why you'd done what you did?"

My eyes flicked back to his, and I relaxed at the warm smile on his face. "What?" I asked, needing to know and yet worried it wouldn't be the answer I wanted to hear.

"I thought you were brave. A little crazy, but mostly brave. And I felt awed that you put yourself at risk to ensure the safety of your family. That's something I understand, and it made me feel like I already knew you."

I blinked at him, stunned by the sweetness of his words. For the first time today, I was glad about what had happened.

I had a feeling that if I'd met my mate any other day, I'd have dragged him to my bed and had my way with him. But now, because of my injuries, I was talking to him instead, and it felt good. It felt right.

Always have a plan, don't you, Fate? I thought to myself, shaking my head at their mechanizations.

"Thank you," I whispered, realizing I'd never said anything after Harlan's sweet words.

He smiled at me and pushed my hair back from my face. A knock at the door stopped him from saying whatever he was about to, and I called out for the person to come in.

"Hey, Nox. How are you doing?" Reece asked as he walked up to me, his brown eyes warm as he looked me over.

"Peachy," I said with a grin, and he rolled his eyes before placing his palm on my chest. I winced at the slight pain it caused, and Reece gave me an apologetic look as his magic started working.

"Sorry. I think it'll take another few rounds before you're completely healed, but this one should heal you enough for some small movements. You can sit up in bed, walk a little, but nothing more strenuous, got it? If you ruin my hard work, I will leave you half-healed."

I knew better than to doubt his threat, so I merely nodded, excited at the prospect of getting to move around.

"FYI, you have some serious apologizing to do. Arty isn't happy with you, and neither is Zane, and they can hold a grudge better than anyone."

"Oh, don't I know it? They came by, called me an asshole, and then haven't returned since." I smiled wryly. While I knew Zane was legendary at holding onto their anger, I also knew their weakness. In fact, I was friends with him. Wren would get me out of this pickle; I was sure of it.

"Sounds like Zane," Reece said with a chuckle. A few minutes later, he was done with this round, and I felt much better. My muscles weren't as stiff, and I could move around if I did it slowly.

"I can heal you more, but I need to reserve some magic in case someone else gets hurt," Reece said with an apologetic smile, and I patted his hand since it was still on my chest.

"It's okay. I understand. Don't worry about it, okay? I've got some great company," I said, my eyes flicking to Harlan, who leaned against the wall beside the bed so he'd be out of Reece's way but still close enough to help.

Reece grinned and squeezed my hand. "I'm happy for you. I'll see you in a few hours, okay?"

"See ya." As he left, I turned to Harlan and gave him my best puppy eyes. "Help me up, please? I want to sit."

Harlan

My mate really was like a little child. Because once he was seated, I had to stop him from trying to leave the bed every five minutes. And since he was naked under the sheets—Reece had removed his pants so he could see his injuries, and apparently, my mate liked going commando—I kept getting peeks of his gorgeous pale skin every time. He looked gorgeous despite all the burns on his body, and I had to tamp down my attraction because he wasn't healed enough for what I wanted to do to him.

"I just need my phone. I need to talk to Wren," Nox grumbled, and I rolled my eyes.

"Tell me where it is, and I'll get it for you."

He made a face and waved around the room. "Somewhere, probably. I don't use it much."

I shook my head and bit back a smile as I stood up and walked over to his dresser. The top was bare, but the cabinets were an explosion of color that had me raising a brow as I sifted through the clothes.

I heard Nox swear under his breath before he spoke louder, saying, "Oh, you know what? It's all right. I'll text him later. Why don't you come back here?"

The only reason I didn't make a teasing remark was because I could hear the nerves in his voice. I ran my palm over the purple satin gown at the top of his clothes before turning to him. "These are yours, aren't they?"

I watched as his Adam's apple bobbed, and he blew out a breath before nodding. "Yeah. I don't... I don't wear them outside."

"Why not? I bet you look beautiful in them."

His cheeks turned pink, and he stared at his lap, playing with the sheets as he avoided my gaze. This version of him was so different from the smartass brat I'd been talking to until now that it took me a moment to change gears. This was a side of Nox I doubted many got to see, and I had a feeling I needed to be careful in what I said to him.

"But, if you prefer to only wear them indoors, then I hope I'll be able to earn the privilege of seeing you in them," I said, and a small smile crept onto his face.

I closed the cabinet door and walked over to a window seat that looked like the perfect reading spot. I found his phone half-buried under a pile of pillows and pulled it out, handing it to him before resuming my seat.

"Thanks," he murmured, shooting me a bright smile as he unlocked the phone. The smile disappeared as he saw something, a grimace replacing it instead.

"Everything okay?" I asked, feeling an irrational urge to take his phone away from him.

"Yeah. Everyone's just really worried, and kinda mad, I guess. I hate that I've troubled everyone so much."

I took his free hand in mine, glad I could touch him without causing him pain now. "Everything will be fine, okay? You'll be all healed up in a day or so, and then the others won't have anything to worry about."

"I guess. Hey, where's my staff? And my cloak?" He looked around the room, searching for them.

"They're in the living room, I think. Let me check."

I squeezed his hand and left the bedroom, looking around the living room. When I'd brought Nox in, I hadn't spared it more than a glance, and when Damien had asked me to step out so he could talk to Nox, I'd been too worried about him to look around much.

Now that I did, I could see Nox's touch everywhere. There were pillows on the couch with silk covers, a bright pink throw on the back that looked like satin, a hodgepodge of furniture that didn't seem to match but fit together well. It was eclectic, and very Nox.

I spotted his staff leaning against the wall near a bookshelf, the cloak hanging on a coat rack. I grabbed both, sensing Nox's magic in the staff. It was strong, and it seemed to greet me like it recognized who I was. I sent a bit of my magic into the staff, and a warm feeling washed over me, a weird contentment I'd never felt before.

I headed back to the bedroom and frowned when I saw the door was closed. When had I closed it?

I turned the knob, frowning when it didn't budge. What the hell?

"Nox?" I called, and I wasn't sure, but I thought I heard some shuffling on the other side. "Nox, open the door, please."

"Go away," he shot back, and I raised my brows. What the fuck? What just happened?

"What's going on, Nox?"

"I want you to leave me alone! Go!" Nox shouted, banging at the door once as if to show me he meant it before I heard him moving away.

I didn't understand. What had changed in the time it'd taken me to grab his stuff? Why was Nox doing this?

SIX

Nox

The moment Harlan left the room to get my staff, I hurried out of bed. Or, well, I tried to before realizing slow and steady was the way to go.

I wanted to see for myself what damage I'd taken. The pain told me it was extensive, but I needed to see it.

Stumbling over to my dresser, I rested my palms on top of it before taking a deep breath and looking up into the mirror. A gasp of horror slipped past my lips as I took myself in, my eyes roaming over my naked body in all its burned glory.

I'd always prided myself on my good looks. I wasn't arrogant about it—I hoped—but I knew I was good-looking, and I enjoyed feeling pretty. But I didn't look pretty right now. I looked downright ugly.

And I'd looked worse when Harlan had first seen me. The realization knocked the breath out of me, and then I was rushing to my bedroom door and closing it. I turned the knob, locking Harlan out before I pressed my forehead to the wood and groaned.

If this was how Harlan saw me, would he even find me attractive? I remembered the way I'd flirted with him earlier, when I'd told Damien I wanted to climb Harlan like a tree, and humiliation washed through me. Harlan must've been disgusted imagining that scenario with me looking the way I did.

What if Reece couldn't heal me completely? What if this was how I'd look now? I didn't want to be ugly.

I shouted at Harlan to leave me alone when he kept knocking, hurrying over to my dresser and grabbing one of my simpler robes to cover myself with because I couldn't bear to keep looking down at the mess that was my once-gorgeous body.

Once I'd covered myself up, I crawled back onto my bed, resting my forehead on my knees and wrapping my arms around my legs. This wasn't how it was supposed to go. I was supposed to find my mate and live happily ever after.

I'd dreamed about it for so long, wishing every day that it would be the one when I finally found them. Even when I'd been with Zane, I'd secretly hoped for it. And when Zane had found their mate, I'd been happy for them, but also extremely jealous. Zane had never shown any interest in finding their mate, and yet they'd found Wren before I found my mate. How was that fair?

Yet now that I had my mate, I'd locked him out of my room because I couldn't bear for him to see me this way. Not that he hadn't already, but now that I knew what I looked like, it felt worse.

"Nox, open up!" My head shot up at the voice that definitely wasn't Harlan, and I shook my head. He'd called Zane? Seriously?

"Go away!" I shouted, and there were some low murmurs on the other side that I couldn't quite understand.

"You do know that I can come in, right? You haven't removed my signature yet." The lock to my room opened with magical signatures, and other than me, only the royal three and Zane could unlock it. Fuck, I knew I should've removed their signature.

"I don't want to see anyone," I grumbled, knowing they'd hear it with their super-sensitive hearing.

"Well, tough luck, because I'm coming in." And they did, the very next second. I curled up tighter as I waited for Harlan to follow them in, but he didn't. Zane closed the door behind them before walking closer to me. "What's the deal? Why did you lock him out?" Their eyes narrowed as their fangs peeked out, and they growled, "Did he hurt you?"

"What? No! Nothing like that. He's been great," I said, my eyes unwilling to meet theirs. Zane had a way of reading me that was uncannily accurate, and I didn't want them to see the embarrassment and humiliation that was drowning me right now, making my skin feel clammy and itchy when I could get neither as a courtesy of being a soul.

"Then what is it?" they asked, coming to sit at the edge of my bed.

I sighed, knowing Zane well enough to know they wouldn't leave until they had their answers.

"I looked into the mirror," I admitted, sneaking a glance at them to see surprise flicker across their features.

"You know this is temporary, right? Reece will heal you soon enough."

"I know that. But this is how Harlan first saw me. What if, even when I'm healed, this is all he can see when he looks at me? What if he's disgusted by me?"

Even as I said the words, some part of me knew they didn't make complete sense, but I didn't care. I'd never felt like this before. I felt insecure about a lot of things, but never my appearance. I prided myself on my body because even if I was a little fucked-up on the inside, my body made up for it. Or it had, until now.

"What if it's a good thing?" Zane countered, and I glared at them.

"In what world could this be a good thing?" I growled, and they smiled as if they thought I was being cute.

"In the world where you have a tendency of using your body to keep people at bay," they said, and I blinked at them.

"What do you mean?"

"I mean... Nox, you're a great guy, okay? But whenever we were together, I felt like you were always holding back. Like whenever we started going deeper than surface attraction, you'd, well, you'd use sex to drag us back firmly into the sex-only zone. Maybe that was just because you didn't want to feel anything for someone who wasn't your mate, or maybe it was more than that. Either way, these injuries will give Harlan the opportunity to break some of your walls that I never could."

I snapped my mouth shut as they stopped talking, my mind whirling. Had I really done that? I couldn't remember consciously thinking about it, but like I'd said, Zane was great at reading me.

"But... I don't want Harlan to see me like this."

"Well, it might be a little late for that seeing as how he's already seen you. And for what it's worth, the first time I saw Wren, he was stick-thin, dirty, in his fifties, and had my knife sticking out of his neck. A knife *I* threw at him. It didn't affect my feelings for him. At all. And if he can love me after what I did to him, trust me—your temporary injuries aren't going to affect Harlan's feelings for you. He might think you're stupid for what you did, but he isn't going to feel anything but care and adoration for you. Trust me."

Wow, Wren really had changed Zane. Or more like unlocked the sweet, caring side of them none of us had known existed.

"Wow. Am I going to turn into a sappy shit like you now?" I asked, and Zane rolled their eyes.

"I'm leaving, and I'm sending Harlan in. Behave."

"Yes, boss," I said, and Zane shook their head before stalking out of the room, closing the door behind them.

I took a deep breath and waited for my mate to come back to me.

Harlan

I shot to my feet as Zane exited Nox's room, running my fingers through my hair as I waited for them to speak.

"You can go in now," they said, and I frowned.

"Is he okay? Did I do something to upset him?" I asked. I'd spent the past few minutes going over everything that had happened since I met Nox in an attempt to figure out where I'd messed up, but I couldn't for the life of me think of anything.

"You should talk to him," Zane said, and with a finger wave, they left the cabin. I sighed, picking up the cloak and staff I'd placed on the couch before bracing myself and heading back into Nox's bedroom.

Nox was sitting up in bed, his arms wrapped around his knees, a pale pink robe covering him. His eyes followed me as I walked over to a cloak stand in the corner of the room and hung his cloak there, leaning the staff against it.

He stayed silent as I resumed my seat at his bedside, and I returned his steady gaze, waiting for him to say something.

"I'm sorry," he whispered softly, and I leaned forward, resting my forearms on the edge of the bed. I wanted to climb in with him and hold him to me, but the way he'd curled in on himself warned me to keep away.

"It's okay. Can you tell me what happened? Did I do something?"

Nox shook his head, his gray eyes reflecting a sadness I didn't want him to feel. I wanted the mischievous light back in them.

"No, you didn't do anything. It was all me. I saw myself in the mirror, and I freaked out," he explained, and the puzzle pieces finally fell into place.

Nox was gorgeous, despite the burns all over his body. He had a slim, lithe figure, stunning gray eyes, and honey-brown hair with that unique white streak. But more than that, it was his wicked sense of humor and sass that I found attractive.

"I can't imagine how that must've felt. I want to ask you something, but you can always say no," I said, unable to resist when he looked so... defeated.

He gave me a wary look, his arms tightening around his legs before he loosened them with a wince. "Okay?"

"Can I hold you?" I asked, and he blinked, looking stunned. His lips moved without forming words before he dipped his head in the slightest nod.

Carefully, I climbed into the bed beside him and wrapped an arm around his shoulder, pulling him into my side as he dropped his hold on his legs and spread them out on the bed.

I turned to him, tipping his face up so I could look into his eyes. "I won't tell you how to feel, Nox. All I know is that I already care about you. I mean, I jumped into the Burning Chasm for you. I don't do that for just anyone, you know?"

A laugh slipped past Nox's lips, and I smiled in relief. I ran my thumb across his jaw before pulling away, instead taking his hand in mine. "You'll be all healed up in a few days, and then I'll show you exactly how much I like you. But until then, how about you and I get to know each other a bit better, huh? And you can tell me all about Otherworld. There's still so much I don't know about my new home."

Nox watched me for a long moment, his gray eyes gazing into the depths of my soul. "You really don't mind all of this?" he asked, waving at himself.

"I mind that you got hurt, Nox, nothing else. I wish I'd been there with you, or that I'd shown up a few minutes sooner so I could've saved you from the pain."

"You did save me, Harlan. I never thanked you for it, did I?"

"You didn't have to. All you need to do is rest and heal up, okay?"

He smiled at me and squeezed my hand. "Deal."

SEVEN

Nox

If all went well, this would be my last healing session with Reece. Most of my burns had healed up, and only a few scars on my chest and arms were left. They'd been deeper, and Reece had been slowly healing them a little in each session.

"Remember, you still have to stay away from the Chasm," Harlan said, a brow raised as if he knew exactly where my mind was.

"I know, I know. Trust me, no matter how reckless I was, I do have a little self-preservation."

"I'll believe it when I see it," Harlan said with a smirk, and I was just about to snap back a decidedly sassy reply when there was a knock at the door.

Harlan—who still wouldn't let me walk around much, even though I was almost completely healed—hurried over to the door and opened it, but instead of Reece, a six-year-old cannonball shot into the room, jumping on the couch beside me as his eyes roamed over me.

"Are you okay, Nox? Dad said you did something *phenomenally* stupid and got hurt," Walker said, eyes widening as he saw the last of the burns on my arms. He was an adorable little kid, and I hated that I'd worried him too.

"Your Dad is a worrywart, kiddo. I'm okay. Your Da will heal me right up, don't you worry," I assured him. I'd known what I'd done had been *phenomenally* stupid, but until now, the full implications of it hadn't quite sunk in. But seeing the worry on Walker's little face made me realize just how big of a risk I'd taken. I could've lost this hodgepodge family of mine forever. Why had I risked that?

To protect them. That was the only reason I'd done it. I'd needed to find out what the queen's plan was so I could keep my family safe. But if this experience had taught me anything, it was that to protect my family, I actually needed to *be* here. Be alive-ish.

"Ready?" Reece asked, and I blinked back to the present. I hadn't even noticed him follow Walker in, but now he sat on the couch on my other side.

"Yep. I'm ready to get back to work," I declared, rolling my eyes when Harlan huffed. He was so protective, and honestly, I loved it. Not that I'd tell *him* that. I liked acting like it annoyed me, but it felt good to have someone's sole focus be my well-being. My Otherworld family loved me, but they had others they cared about more.

Except Lionel. Damn, I needed to go see him once I was done here. After Zane had found Wren, Lionel and I had bonded over the fact that we were the only two left without mates in the inner circle. Caelan was a unique case because while he'd found his mate, he wouldn't be doing anything about it for another dozen years at least. But now that I'd found Harlan, I wanted to make sure Lionel didn't feel lonely.

"All right, we're done!" Reece declared after a few minutes, and I turned to him, taking his hands in mine.

"Thank you so much, Reece. For everything."

"No problem. Just don't do anything so reckless again, or I might be tempted to leave you to your fate, got it?"

"No more recklessness, I promise."

"I'll take care of him, Reece. Don't worry," Harlan chipped in, and I shot him a narrow-eyed gaze even as butterflies fluttered in my belly.

"I can take care of myself now, thank you very much." He merely winked at me, and I shook my head, turning back to Reece.

"Can I join in on the meetings at the very least? And who is taking care of the Chasm right now?"

"Yes, you can come to the meetings. There's one in an hour. And Lionel volunteered to do it after Zane picked up your staff and cloak. And he'll continue to do it for at least the next two weeks, and you're not to try to go there before then."

"I won't try to stay or work, but I do need to talk to Lionel. I don't want him to feel abandoned," I said, flicking a glance to Harlan. When Zane had found Wren, they'd disappeared overnight, and I'd felt like shit. Of course, Zane and my relationship had been a lot different than my friendship with Lionel, but I still wanted to make sure he knew I'd still be there for him.

"Of course. He would've come to visit, they all would've, but Day told them to let you get better first," Reece said with a smile, and I grinned.

"Can I go play with Kitty now? He'll be gone soon like always, and I don't wanna waste any time I have," Walker asked, and Reece smiled at him as he offered him his hand.

"Sure thing, kiddo. Let's go." To me, he said, "I'll see you later. Take it easy, okay?"

I nodded and waved at Walker as he left.

"Who, or should I say what, is Kitty?" Harlan asked as he settled beside me, and I smiled, though it was tinged with sadness for my friend.

"Kitty is Walker's nickname for Damien's best friend Caelan. Caelan doesn't live with us anymore since he discovered Walker was his mate," I explained, and Harlan's brows shot up. "Yeah, exactly. Caelan didn't want Walker to think he'd been grooming him or something, so he left Otherworld. He came back because of all the danger, but once we're through this, he'll probably leave again."

"I imagine it was hard for him to stay away when Walker was in danger," Harlan said, and I nodded.

"Exactly. And I think Walker senses their connection on some level because he's trusted Caelan since the beginning, and Walker doesn't trust easily."

"I got that when he didn't spare me more than a glance," Harlan said with a chuckle, and I smiled.

"He doesn't trust Lionel either, though that's probably because of how awkward he gets around Walker. That reminds me—I need to talk to Lionel. Would you like to come with me?" I offered, though I kind of wanted to talk to Lionel alone first, and I wanted to do it now before I let something else distract me.

He gave me a speculative look before shaking his head. "Nah, you go ahead. Though... I know he's at the Chasm right now, so could you maybe ask him to meet you somewhere else? I really don't want you near that place right now."

It seemed like an okay compromise to me, so I nodded and texted Lionel to meet me in the garden behind the villa. He texted back instantly, assuring me he'd be there.

"Okay, we're meeting in the garden behind the villa. What will you be doing?"

"I wanted to visit Wren, actually. Thank him for helping me get you. He's also the only other warlock here, so I thought I'd talk magic with him."

"Sounds good. Be careful with Wren, okay? He's... he's a gentle soul," I said, not sure how else to phrase it. It was accurate enough, though, so I left it at that.

"I will," Harlan assured me, and I didn't doubt him.

Harlan

I found Wren in the lounge of the Brume Villa, where the king, his family, and the chiefs of Otherworld lived with their mates. I hadn't asked Nox why he didn't live here with the rest of them, but I suspected it had something to do with the cabin's proximity to the Chasm, and I wasn't sure I liked that idea.

Wren sat cross-legged on an armchair, his head buried in a book, his black curls hiding his face from anyone who passed by. The only reason I knew it was him was because I could sense his magic.

"Wren?" I said softly, not wanting to startle him.

He glanced up at me, eyes widening a little when he saw me. Hesitantly, he waved at me, and I smiled as I walked closer to him and took a seat on the couch across from him.

"Hey, Wren. I just wanted to thank you again for helping me get Nox back. I couldn't have done it without you."

He dipped his head with a small smile, not saying a word. Come to think of it, I hadn't heard him say a word, not even when he was doing the portal spell. Could he not speak at all?

"Uh, I thought that since we're both warlocks, and we seem to be the only ones who retained our powers, there must be a reason for it, don't you think? Nox said there was another man—Kym, I think?—who got his powers after coming to Otherworld. Do you think it's all connected?"

Wren blinked at me, his teeth abusing his lower lip for a long moment before he sighed and grabbed the notepad and pen that sat on the coffee table in front of him.

I watched as he scrawled on the paper, his brows furrowed in concentration. After a minute, he brandished the notepad at me.

I think so, too. Kym has the power to purify a soul, though he can't use it on more than one soul without exhausting himself. I don't know why I was allowed to keep my magic. I don't even remember any spells other than the portal spell.

I frowned at the last sentence, confused about what he meant. "Weren't you formally trained when you were younger?"

He dipped his head, which I took to mean he had been trained. He wrote something else on the notepad before showing it to me.

I was held captive for a while before I got here. They only needed me to do the portal spell every time they wanted to escape. While I was held, I forgot the other spells since I didn't have a chance to use them.

I blinked at the words, horrified at the implication. Warlocks, like witches, had been persecuted for a long time. Unlike mages, whose magic came from the elements, we had our own magic that we could modify with the potions and spells we used. And having our own magic made us more powerful, which in turn gave others the incentive to either hunt us down or capture us for their own good. While my sister and I had spent our lives avoiding the first, it seemed Wren had been prey to the latter.

"I'm sorry you had to go through that. If you want, I'd be happy to teach you any spells you wish to learn," I offered, and his eyes widened.

The notepad he held started shaking, and before I could ask him if he was okay, Zane appeared beside him, instantly stepping between us as I leaned back to give them some space.

Zane spoke softly to Wren, but all I could hear was soft murmurs. They'd blocked my view of Wren, but I just hoped he was okay.

I debated leaving them to it, but my conversation with Wren hadn't ended, and I didn't want him to think I'd left because I didn't want to help him.

After a few minutes, Zane leaned forward and kissed Wren, gave him a hug, and stood up. They nodded at me before returning their gaze to their mate. "I'll be back in a few to get you for the meeting, okay?"

"Thank you." The words were so soft-spoken I thought I'd imagined them, but then Zane smiled brightly, something I'd never seen them do in the short time I'd known them.

"You're welcome, sweetie." Then Zane was gone as I tried to comprehend the fact that Wren could speak. Was it anxiety then, that kept him from talking to me?

Wren blinked at me, a wary expression on his face like he wasn't sure where to go from here, so I gave him a reassuring smile. He smiled back hesitantly before writing some more on his notepad.

Sorry about that. ~~I just don't~~ I haven't used magic for any-thing else in a long time, and I just panicked. Sorry.

"It's okay, Wren. You don't have to learn if you don't want to."

He shook his head, his pace more frantic as he flipped the page and started writing.

No, I need to. There's a reason there are two warlocks here. You have to teach me.

"Okay, if you say so. How about you, me, Zane, and Nox get together later and figure something out?" I asked, and the relief on his face was hard to miss.

He nodded instantly, and I smiled. "I think I have your number, so I'll text you once I've talked to Nox. That okay?" When I'd first woken up here, Zane had given me a phone that was specially made so it could be used in Otherworld and the human realm. Nox had then added everyone's contact information in it in a fit of boredom, so now I had the numbers of people I hadn't even met yet.

He nodded again, and I grinned. "Perfect."

Zane reappeared just then, their eyes immediately latching onto their mate. "It's time for the meeting." Then they turned to me, "You should come too. You're part of this now."

I was, wasn't I? In the last two years, this was the second family that had accepted me as one of theirs. And while I'd never felt like I fit in Mistvale, I fit here, among these people. Otherworld was home.

EIGHT

Nox

I found Lionel perched on a tree branch in the garden behind the villa, and he waved at me when he spotted me, shooting up into the air before flying down to me. The show-off.

"Hey, man. You're looking much better," he said as he pushed his chestnut hair back. It still felt... different to see it in its true color, since he'd spent so long keeping it platinum. The feathers of his white wings—that made him look like the angel he definitely wasn't—fluttered in the light breeze, their tips glowing softly in the sunlight. While Damien's wings were midnight black and gorgeous in their own rights, Lionel's were the complete opposite, though just as beautiful.

"Did everyone see me in my crispy glory?" I demanded, and he chuckled.

"Pretty much. Except Walker, of course."

I blew out a breath. I really had made a giant fool of myself in front of everyone, hadn't I?

"So, how are you doing?" I asked, and Lionel shrugged.

"Same as usual."

"I was just worried," I said, not sure how to address the elephant in the... garden? Thankfully, Lionel did it for me.

"Because you have a mate now and I'm the only one left without one?" he asked, and I ducked my head, scratching the back of my neck. "Don't you worry about me. I'm sure I'm next."

The confidence in his voice made me look up, and I raised a brow at him. "Oh?"

"After years of no one finding their mates, over the past few years, four of us have found our mates. There's a very good chance I'm next, so I'm going to stick with that hope until I'm proven right," he declared, and I smiled. Lionel's unending optimism was just one of the things I liked about him. He was a great friend, and it made me feel slightly guilty that if I'd found my mate early on, I might never have grown so close to him.

It took Lionel a while to act normal around people. He had an awkward streak that made it hard for him to make small talk or talk to someone he'd never met before. But once I'd gotten past that layer, I'd realized he was a really great guy.

"Oh, hey. I heard you were the one who brought Harlan home. Thank you for that," I said, honestly grateful, and Lionel grinned.

"He's perfect for you. A keeper for the keeper," Lionel declared, and my cheeks went warm. He was kinda perfect, wasn't he?

"Oh my Afterworld, you're blushing!" Lionel gasped, a wide smile on his face, and I glared at him even as my cheeks darkened.

"I'm not. Take that back!"

"You are! Oh my, this is so cute. *You* are so cute!"

"Stop. Talking!" I demanded, and Lionel jumped back as I went to smack him, taking off at a run, his wings folded tightly against his back, as if he was worried I'd try to grab them. I chased after him for a while before the bastard cheated and took off into the air. I wished I had wings.

"See you at the meeting!" he shouted before flying into the direction of the office building. I shook my head at him as I took a moment to just soak in the fact that I was here. In Otherworld. I'd made it.

I'd gone into the Burning Chasm, found the information I'd been looking for, and I'd come back.

Of course, if I'd worked with my family like I should've, I wouldn't have returned as a crisp potato, but you learn something every day, right?

I wasn't sure if Harlan would be at the meeting or not, if anyone had told him, so I went to the lounge first, since that was where Wren usually was this time of the day. It was part of his therapy, to spend some time in a semi-public location every day. We had strict orders from Zane to not initiate contact unless Wren did it, but I'd broken it more than once when I'd felt like he needed someone to talk to, and it'd always paid off. Just because Zane was his mate didn't mean they always knew what was best for him. No one could *always* know that.

Neither of them were in the lounge, but I saw one of the notepads Wren used sitting on the coffee table, the top few pages torn off. Zane had a habit of doing that, and it was equal parts adorable and overprotective AF. It wasn't like anyone would try to peek into Wren's private conversation. Wren—whether he knew it or not—was mated to the scariest person in the realm, and no one who valued their second life would ever dare to harm him in any way.

I hoped they'd taken Harlan with them when they went to the meeting.

Oh, wait. I could just text Harlan and ask him.

Except, when I patted my pockets, I came up empty. No phone anywhere. Damn it.

Sighing, I headed to the conference room, deciding I'd use someone else's phone if Harlan wasn't there.

I spotted him the moment I stepped into the room. He was talking to Vaishnavi, the chair beside him empty. The meeting hadn't started yet, so I tuned into their conversation as I sat down, groaning when I realized it was about me.

"So then, after Nox stood in front of the Burning Chasm for a whole day wearing nothing but a lacy thong, Damien got him the cloak he now wears. Its magic keeps him from heating up," she was saying, and Harlan had a wide-ass grin on his face.

"Vee! Don't ruin my image in front of my mate," I hissed, to which she merely raised a brow at me.

"You mean the image you created when he had to rescue you from a soul-destroying fire?"

I flushed bright red, though unlike earlier, this time it was solely because of shame. The more time passed, the more I regretted what I'd done, not just because of the impression I'd made on Harlan, but because of what I'd put my family through. Because even though Vaishnavi's words were teasing, her deep brown eyes reflected nothing but concern and worry, and that was how it'd been with everyone in my family. I'd worried them all, and that was the last thing I'd ever wanted to do.

A warm, callused palm squeezed my hand, and I looked up into warm blue eyes. Harlan smiled softly and said, "It's okay, Nox."

I nodded slowly, turning back to the others as Damien took his seat at the head of the table, smiling at me when he met my eyes. I returned his smile and straightened in my chair. What had happened was done, but now I needed to buckle up and help my family take down the evil that was trying to destroy everything we stood for. And I'd do it with my mate by my side.

Harlan

Watching them work together was fascinating. There were a *lot* of people here. There was Vaishnavi, who sat beside me and was the Chief of Macaria's Children, responsible for sending children's souls to Afterworld—except for that one time when Walker had somehow chosen to stay in Otherworld. Beside her was her mate, Mazia. She was the chief of Februus's Coop, collecting the souls of all the non-criminal adults who weren't heroes. Normal people.

There was Zane and Wren, Maximus and his mate Kym, the king and his two mates, Artemus and Reece. There was a man with huge white wings who I assumed was Lionel. And the last person, sitting beside Reece, was Caelan. His cat ears twitched every few seconds, and claw-like nails tapped the desk, showing his agitation even though he hadn't uttered a word otherwise.

There were so many people, and it should've felt crowded and messy, and yet they all worked together so seamlessly. Like a family.

"So, this is what we have till now: The Queen of Underworld—whose name we don't know—"

"Meredith," Artemus cut in, and Damien shook his head.

"Of course, you know. Meredith is such a... nice name. I thought her name would be something fitting. Like Cruella," Damien mused, and I bit back a chuckle, though the others didn't.

"The wicked witch of the Chasm?" Caelan suggested with a straight face, and Nox chuckled beside me.

"Ooh, what about Maleficent?" he suggested, and Damien grinned wryly before raising a palm.

"Okay, okay, let's not get sidetracked. So, the queen of Underworld wants our realm. She has five supes in the human realm she has infected with some potion so five of her... followers could jump into their bodies and help her create more hosts for the other souls of the Chasm. Meredith intends to take over Otherworld once she has broken out of the Chasm. Somehow, she has managed to dig deeper into the Chasm and escape the fires, so the souls are not as weak as they should've been. Is that all?"

"I'm confident we've cleared all of their followers from the human realm, but the problem is that we can't hold them in the magical prisons Reece created for long. If they escape, they might be able to help the others escape from the Chasm. We might need to risk sending them into the Chasm," Maximus said, and Nox stiffened beside me.

"But the Chasm isn't working anymore," he protested, and Maximus grimaced.

"Trust me, I know. It's not ideal, but the Chasm is still a better prison than what we have here."

"How about we hold back Cynthia's soul, since the witch is one of the more powerful players in this? The rest, we can send into the Chasm," Damien said, and there were murmurs of agreement.

"I'll work on creating a permanent shield around the Chasm, coded to our auras, so only a select few people can go close to it," Reece said, and I glanced at him.

"I can help with that. I know a few shielding spells that could be helpful," I said, and Wren raised his hand as if to say he'd like to help too.

Reece smiled and nodded at me and Wren. "Thanks, that would be great."

"After that, our next step has to be finding these supes. Maximus, have your contacts in the realm look for them. Focus on supes who live solitary lives, who don't have people who'd notice if they disappeared. Nox, did she say if she was holding them captive, or if they'd just been infected?"

Nox's brows furrowed as he thought about the conversation. "I'm pretty sure she said they were free, that they were living the last days of their lives without knowing what was to come."

"That makes this much more complicated," Damien muttered, and I had to agree. If only we knew if there was an indicator...

I sat up as a thought crossed my mind, and I spoke before the thought had completely formed. "Maximus, Zane, you fought a pack of rabid shifters recently, didn't you? The ones you rescued the kids from?"

Zane glanced at Wren before nodding at me, and I turned to Nox. "And Nox, the queen mentioned something about us killing her first batch or experiments or something, didn't she?"

"She did," Nox said slowly, as if trying to figure out where I was going with this.

I turned back to the others, hoping I could explain this right. "So, what if those shifters were the first ones to drink the potion that would make them the hosts? Max, Zane, did you notice anything different about their auras? Anything that set them apart from the rest of the souls?"

Maximus scratched his beard as he thought, and his eyes shot to mine a minute later. "Inky black."

"Uh, what?" Nox asked, and Maximus looked around the room.

"At that time, I kept thinking their souls were black as ink. I didn't realize back then how it wasn't quite the same as the other dark souls. Usually, even the darkest of souls have a more... smoky aura, but these shifters had auras that were oppressively dark, thick like oil or ink. At the time, I assumed it was because of the blood they'd drunk, because that's what the kids and Wren thought they were drinking."

"But it was actually the potion," Nox continued. "And now all we need to do is look for people with similar auras." He turned to me, his gray eyes glowing like molten silver as he grinned. "Holy fuck, Harlan! You figured it out!"

And then, in front of everyone, Nox kissed me. My mate kissed me. The only man I'd ever been with—a fact I'd been trying to find the right time to share with him, not that it changed anything—kissed me. And I loved every second of it.

NINE

Nox

In some distant part of my brain, I remembered that we weren't alone, but the moment my lips touched Harlan's, everything else just disappeared.

His kiss was full of hesitation and sweetness, his lips soft against mine as he did his best to keep the kiss chaste while I did my best to make it very not-chaste.

It was the sound of whistles and cheers that finally had me pulling back, and I grinned as Harlan blushed a deep red all the way to the tops of his ears. I hadn't thought Harlan could look adorable, but here it was. With a sheepish smile on his face and a blush coloring his cheeks, cute was the only word I could think of to describe him.

"You two are seriously adorable," Kym called from the other side of the table, and I grinned at him, bowing my head to accept the compliment.

"That they are. But let's not get too sidetracked. Harlan's theory has merit, but it also means that your human realm contacts won't be able to help. You'll need to get your and

Zane's squad on this, since they're the only ones who have seen what these auras look like. Every person you can spare needs to be scouring the realm for them. Start with where you found the shifter pack, and work your way outwards. Any questions?" Damien asked, and everyone shook their heads. It was a simple plan, but it was what we needed right now. If all went well, we'd soon secure those supes.

Once the meeting dispersed, I followed Harlan out of the room. I'd been so excited to get better so I could do all the things I wanted to do to Harlan, but now that I was healed, I couldn't get what Zane had said out of my head. Had I really used sex as a way to keep them at a distance? But they were one of my closest friends.

I didn't want to do the same with Harlan. I wanted to let him in. I wanted him to see every part of me, even the slightly fucked-up ones.

"Did anyone show you around Otherworld yet?" I asked as we stepped out of the building we'd ingeniously dubbed the *office building*.

"Well, you kinda interrupted my last tour, and then I was busy with more important things, so no," Harlan said, a teasing glint in his eyes, and I grinned.

Taking his hand in mine, I tugged him toward the village. The others didn't spend a lot of time in the village, but I loved going there. Since I didn't get to leave Otherworld because of my job, I loved hearing stories about the human realm from the other residents of Otherworld.

"This," I said, waving around at the mismatch of cabins, huts, and modern houses, "is the village. This is where all the other soul collectors live."

Harlan nodded as he looked around, his lower lip caught between his teeth. "Zane mentioned finding me a home here."

"Well, you won't need it anymore, but later, I'll introduce you to some of my favorite people here," I said, and he blinked at me.

"Why won't I need a house?"

My brows furrowed, and it took me a minute to realize what he meant. "Uh, because you'll be living with me? Since we're mates?"

"Oh," Harlan said, not sounding a bit enthusiastic about the prospect, not like I was.

I looked down, feeling foolish about the assumption I'd made. "Sorry. If you don't want to stay with me, that's okay. There are always a few cabins empty here."

I scraped my shoe against the rocky ground, wishing it'd open up and swallow me whole. Instead, warm fingers pressed against my chin, and I reluctantly met Harlan's eyes as he tilted my face up.

"Nox, I'd love to stay with you," he said, his voice soft and clear and honest. "I was just surprised, because... " He trailed off, and I raised my brow at him.

"Because?" I asked, placing my palms on his waist as I stepped closer to him.

"Well, because you're the first guy I've ever been with, and I don't want to mess it up." I blinked at him, not having expected that at all. He'd never been with a guy before?

"So... you're attracted to me, right?" Oh fuck, what if he wasn't? But we had to be compatible, right? Fate wouldn't have paired us otherwise.

"Of course I am. You're hot as hell, Nox. I just... I'm a bit clueless about everything, and I hate not knowing things. You'd think having a gay best friend I'd have picked some things up, but nope."

I smiled, seeing this side of him for the first time. Until now, he'd been Harlan: the man who saved my life, my knight, the man who'd sat at my bedside and taken care of me. But now, he was Harlan: my mate, who'd never been with a man and was feeling just a little insecure.

I squeezed his waist and stepped closer to him, my eyes never leaving his as I said, "You have nothing to worry about. Luckily for you, I know everything there is to know about being with a man, and I'd be only too happy to teach you, young padawan."

Harlan chuckled softly, and then as if he couldn't resist, he leaned forward and pressed his lips to mine. I let him lead as he acquainted himself with every inch of my lips, humming at the way our bodies felt pressed together.

"Aw, man! They're everywhere!" We sprang apart at the voice, and I turned to glare at Malik, who merely glared back at me.

"Harlan, this jerk is Malik. He's Maximus's second-in-command. Malik, my mate, Harlan," I introduced as I continued to glare at him for interrupting a perfectly amazing second kiss.

"Nice to meet you, Harlan," Malik said, shooting him a smile before sticking his tongue out at me. "I'll see you later."

Once he was gone, Harlan raised a brow at me. "So what was that about?"

"I'm guessing he walked in on Max and Kym before he came here. Again. Those two have no self control. It makes Malik's job very difficult."

Harlan chuckled softly, using the tips of his fingers to tuck my hair behind my ears, his palms coming to rest on my cheeks as he cupped my face. I shivered at the gentle touch, leaning into it as I gazed up at him. "What about you? Do you have self control?"

"Huh?" I mumbled unintelligently, shaking my head to get it back on track. "Oh yeah, I do. I have all the self control, baby."

Harlan grinned, clearly amused with my declaration. "I guess we'll see, won't we?"

Harlan

"Wait, what?" Nox asked, as if he hadn't heard me. Considering he'd had his head buried under a mound of pillows, I was guessing he really hadn't.

"I said get up and get dressed because we're going on a date."

He sat up, his hair a tangled mess and sleep lines creasing his cheek. Yet he was the most stunning man I'd ever seen. "A date?" he asked, voice full of confusion, as if he'd never heard of the concept.

"You know, when a guy who likes another guy takes him out to have a good time to show him he likes him? A date?" I said, and he rolled his eyes and threw a pillow at me. I caught it before it could hit me, throwing it on the bed before I climbed on to it. "You have the time off, and Damien said I could take a few days before I start working. As for saving the world, we're kind of in a standstill until we find the five supes, so I thought we could take the time to get to know each other better. Unless you don't want to."

Nox's eyes widened, and he scrambled closer to me, taking my hands in his. "Are you kidding? I definitely want to. Give me ten minutes."

"You might wanna wear a shirt too. We're not staying in Otherworld," I added, and his eyes widened.

"We're going to the human realm? Really?"

"Yep," I answered, smiling at the excitement on his face. "I thought you could wear some of your pretty clothes. If you want," I added, nodding toward the cabinet full of colorful clothes.

The excitement on his face turned to apprehension, and I squeezed his hands. "Only if you want to, of course. And if you want it to be just for us, we can leave from right here so the others don't see. There will be people where we're going, just no one we know."

Nox thought for a minute, chewing on his lower lip. I wanted to lean forward and tug it free, but I resisted the urge, letting Nox think it over. "I don't really know why I'm hesitant. I mean, Damien wears clothes like these all the time, and no one's ever said anything to him. Though he's the king, so it's not like anyone would even if they wanted to."

He wasn't wrong about that, but I had a feeling if someone spoke badly of Nox's outfit, they'd find themselves on the bad side of a lot of people, including me.

"It's your choice either way. I know you'd look stunning in anything. I just want you to be comfortable in whatever you wear, okay? I'll wait in the living room." Pressing a soft kiss to his forehead, I slipped out of the bed. In the living room, I perused his bookshelf, seeing a lot of books about the human realm.

Since Nox was the Keeper of the Chasm, it hadn't taken me long to figure out that it'd been a while since he'd been to the human realm. And seeing these books only confirmed the fact that Nox really, really wanted to see the human realm.

I hadn't truly decided where exactly I'd take him in the human realm, since restaurants and cafés were a no-go, but looking at these books gave me some really great ideas, and so I made my plans while I waited for Nox.

When he finally stepped out of the room, I couldn't breathe. Fuck, he was gorgeous.

I stepped closer to him as he nervously tugged at his shirt. It was a pale lavender color, with a glittery ghost on the front. The hem ended at his belly button, and paired with jeans slung low on his hips, the outfits offered a tantalizing peek of his smooth, pale skin.

"Fuck, Nox. You look gorgeous," I murmured, tracing the patch of skin with my fingers because I just couldn't stop myself.

Nox shivered as a grin spread across his face, and as if that was all he'd needed to hear, he was back to his confident, bratty self.

"So? Are we going on this date or what?" he asked, looking up at me with a grin. His lips glistened, and when I pecked them with mine, I realized they tasted of strawberries. I would've gone for another taste, but he pressed his finger to my lips and shook his head.

"Uh-uh, you have to earn more kisses. Show me what this date you've planned is, and maybe I'll let you kiss me."

I chuckled at the declaration, squeezing him to me because I had to do something if I couldn't kiss him.

"All right, here we go," I said, letting my magic take us where I needed to go. Traveling without a portal felt weird, but it was much faster.

When we'd reached our destination, Nox opened his eyes and looked around, frowning when he realized we were in a dark corner behind a structure.

"Well, I couldn't quite let us appear in the middle of a street, could I?" I asked as I took Nox's hand, and he smirked up at me.

"Actually, you could. They can't see us. Not unless we let them, that is."

Huh. I hadn't known that. That made sense, though. I wouldn't want my sister or any of my friends to accidentally catch sight of me if I was ever back in Mistvale.

"Come on, our date awaits." I tugged Nox toward the end of the alley, and he froze the moment we stepped into the light, his eyes widening and a grin spreading across his lips.

"Oh my Afterworld," he breathed, and I knew I'd picked the right place.

TEN

Nox

I actually squealed out loud when I realized where we were, whirling around to grin up at Harlan. "An amusement park? Really?"

He smiled softly, cupping my cheek and rubbing his thumb over my lower lip. "You like it?"

"Fuck yes! I've read about these, but I've never been to one. Damn, I'm so excited!"

I couldn't stand still; that's how excited I was. I pouted when Harlan led us to a line at the gate, and then my eyes widened as he got two VIP tickets for us.

"Where did you get the money from?" I hissed, keeping my voice low.

Harlan shot me a wink as he took our tickets, leading me inside. "Reece. I figured you wouldn't want to spend the majority of our date standing in lines."

I wanted to say I wouldn't mind it if he was with me, but that sounded way too cheesy, so I kept my mouth shut.

"Wait, was that money fake then?" I asked. Reece could make pretty much everything with his magic, so I wouldn't put it past him.

"Reece said he has an account in the bank here, for groceries," he replied, and I shook my head. I'd totally forgotten about that. Reece, Arty, Damien, and Walker were the only ones in Otherworld who actually needed food. Damien hadn't needed it until he'd mated with Reece and Arty, and the running theory was that just like they'd taken parts of his magic, he'd taken parts of their humanity.

"That makes sense." I looked around the place, peering as far as my eyes could go and still not seeing the end of this place. "Holy crap, this place is big. I want to try all the rides!"

"Anything you want. Where would you like to start? Oh, here's the map," Harlan said, unfolding the map he'd been given. We found our location and then mapped out a route that would let us try all the rides. It was a good thing we wouldn't need to waste time on snacks and replenishments, though the air did smell deliciously sweet. Sometimes, I missed food.

"Come on, come on, this way," I said, tugging Harlan with me to the first ride.

It was a ride where you were taken into a cave and got points for shooting the right target. I found two empty seats side by side, and we jumped in. I fiddled with the laser gun and the controls, the screen reading zero points. "Are you any good at shooting?" I asked, and Harlan grinned crookedly.

"I'm better than a ten-year-old, if that's what you're asking," he said, and my brows furrowed before I looked around and realized we were the only adults on the ride.

"Eh, good enough," I said, making him laugh. I grinned at him as the ride started, grabbing the gun with both hands.

The ride was a blast, and Harlan and I had our own little competition over who shot more targets. When we reached the end, my score was the highest, and I whooped loudly, barely resisting the urge to stick my tongue out at the other kids. If that one kid didn't look like Walker, I totally would've.

Instead, I jumped into Harlan's arms, who caught me instantly, and smiled up at him. "We were great, weren't we? We beat them all."

Harlan chuckled, a warm look on his face as he squeezed my waist. "We totally did. Come on, let's go check out the next one before those parents burn us with their glares."

I peeked around him, and sure enough, some of the parents were shooting us narrow-eyed glares, as if we'd somehow committed a crime by enjoying ourselves. Or maybe they were homophobes. In case they were, I leaned up on my toes to press a chaste kiss to Harlan's lips. "Sure, let's go."

Over the next few hours, we tried all types of rides. We knocked into each other with our carts, chased each other with the race cars, and I took that one shot at Harlan's delicious ass with a water gun.

"Let's try the haunted house next!" How scary could it be after my experience in the Burning Chasm?

"Why not? Here it is."

I grinned up at Harlan as the ride started, totally confident it'd be a piece of cake. Until the first jump scare.

I screamed like a banshee, which prompted the other kids on the ride to scream even louder. I wrapped my arms around Harlan's much muscular one, clinging to him for the rest of the ride.

When we got off, a ghost tried to chase me, and I contemplated knocking him out before Harlan dragged me away.

"We will never, ever talk of that again," I declared as soon as we were out of the dark and back on the grounds.

Harlan chuckled. "Why? Because you got a little scared?"

I narrowed my eyes at him before slumping into his side. "Yeah. I didn't get scared like that in the Chasm, and this was a fake human copy of something that doesn't even exist."

"Well technically, aren't we ghosts?" Harlan mused, and I rolled my eyes at him.

"We're soul collectors. Ghosts are those jerks who refuse to come with the soul collectors after their death."

Harlan's brows furrowed. "Does that happen often?"

"Not really. But every once in a while, there's a soul who has a powerful connection to the human realm, usually in the form of some unfinished business. They disappear the moment they get out of their body so the soul collector wouldn't be able to find them. Then they have to wait until the soul is ready to move on before they can try again."

"Huh, I didn't know that. So I guess the ghost stories have some merit after all," he mused, and I smiled, glad we'd moved away from the topic of my fear.

"Come on, I want to try the big roller coaster," I said, taking his hand and pulling him after me.

And then I got my revenge when Harlan freaked out big time as the roller coaster went down, his eyes bulging and his mouth open in a scream, his knuckles white as he gripped the safety belt. I let mine go, spreading my arms wide as I whooped. Leaning toward him, I shouted, knowing my voice would be lost in everyone's screams, "You do know you can't die again, right?"

"I don't care!" he shouted back, and I laughed the rest of the downward ride.

When we finally stumbled off it, Harlan shook his head. "Never. Never again. I feel nauseous, and I can't even puke."

I chuckled at the sulky tone of his voice, wrapping my arms around him. "Aww, did the big bad ride scare my mate?"

He rolled his eyes at me before pulling me to his front. "Are you having fun?"

"Are you kidding me? I can't remember the last time I had so much fun!" I meant it too. Living in Otherworld for so long, taking care of the Chasm day after day, it was all so boring. I hadn't realized how much until I'd gotten a break from it all. The thought of going back to that life seemed scarier than the haunted house ride that had made me want to crap my pants.

Harlan

"Hey, Harlan?" I almost missed the softly spoken words, glancing down at Nox to find him chewing his bottom lip. This time, I did tug it free before tilting his head up.

"What is it?"

He sighed softly, his eyes troubled as he gathered his thoughts. "Do you think Damien would be okay with it if I asked him to get another person to work at the Chasm with me? Two keepers of the Chasm?"

"I don't know Damien as well as you do, but from what I've seen, he thinks of you as his family. I think you should talk to him. Can I ask what brought this on?"

He smiled softly, his arms wrapping around me. "I wasn't lying when I said today was the most fun I've had in a long time, and I just got to thinking that I didn't want to go back to that old life. I'd never minded my job before, but now I know my job has become my whole life, and I don't want that."

"That sounds pretty reasonable to me. I don't think Damien would mind," I told him, and he smiled.

"I'll talk to him tomorrow. For now, let's go on the Ferris wheel. It's giant. I want to kiss you when we get to the top like they do in the movies," he said, his words tumbling over each other as he got excited again.

I grinned and let him drag me to the Ferris wheel, happy my date idea had been so well received. It'd be difficult to one up this next time, but I'd find a way. I wanted to show Nox all the things he'd missed out on, and luckily, I had all the time in the world to do that.

As long as we managed to defeat the queen of Underworld, of course.

As promised, I kissed Nox on top of the Ferris wheel, with the whole park gleaming beneath us. Nox took pictures from his phone, and I smiled as I watched the wide, delighted smile on his face, my chest feeling warm and full of the kind of mushy feelings I'd never, ever experienced before.

"Why do we have to walk to the exit?" Nox complained a few minutes later, hanging onto my arm like he couldn't be bothered to walk on his own.

"Because this place is full of cameras and we don't want one of them catching us suddenly disappearing," I explained, and he blew a raspberry.

"They'll probably think it was a camera malfunction. Humans are very good at making up reasons to explain away the supernatural."

I couldn't disagree with that, but I still thought it was better to stay safe.

When Nox suddenly stopped walking, I thought he'd decided to fuck being safe and was done walking. "Nox—"

"Shh!" he cut me off, his eyes on the crowd in front of us, specifically on a slim, lean man who walked a few feet in front of us.

"What is it?" I asked softly as Nox started dragging me after the man.

"He's one of the five. Text Maximus," Nox said, all the previous lightness gone from his voice.

As he kept his eyes on the supe, I did as he'd asked, sending Maximus our exact location. He told us he'd be there in a minute and to not lose track of the subject.

"They'll be here soon," I murmured softly, and Nox nodded.

We tailed the man as he walked out of the park, his attention solely focused on his phone. After a moment of watching his aura—which was definitely nothing like anything I'd ever seen before, not that I'd had the opportunity to see many of them—I realized he was a wendigo. I'd never seen one before. They were known to be recluses, and while they did consume human flesh, most of them weren't ruthless killers like they were rumored to be.

The man we'd been tailing got into a car, and Nox glanced up at me. "We need to turn invisible so we can follow without raising suspicion. Just think about being invisible and it should happen automatically."

I stared at him dubiously but did as he'd said, and warm magic prickled my skin, telling me it'd worked. It felt different than the magic I was used to using, but it was still mine. My soul collector magic.

Once Nox had turned invisible—to every living soul, not to me—we tailed the car, our magic letting us rush through the streets at speed that allowed us to keep up with the car.

It stopped at a small parking lot at the edge of a camping ground, and the wendigo got out of the car. I felt magic stir beside me and found Maximus and Zane walking up to us. Maximus had a huge sword strapped to his back, and Zane had... way too many knives to count.

"Remember, he's an innocent man," Nox hissed, and Zane raised a brow at him.

"He's a wendigo," Zane pointed out, and I winced. I'd learned it the hard way that you should never, ever judge a supe based on their species. I'd done that with my best friend's mate, judging him for being a half-siren when I'd never even had a proper conversation with him, and my best friend had made it clear exactly how big of an asshole I was for doing that. I'd learned my lesson.

"With a white soul! Look at the darkness. It's nothing like what it was with the shifters. Their souls were rotting. That's how dark they were. But his? It's still fighting. We need to find a way to heal him," Nox hissed, and Zane raised their palms up in surrender.

"First, we need to get him to a safe location. I have a few safe houses in this realm. We'll take him to one of those," Maximus said, and everyone nodded their agreement.

"Now let's go tell him we mean him no harm, with two of us armed to the teeth," Nox said wryly, and Maximus smiled sheepishly.

"Better safe than sorry. Now come on before we lose his trail." I followed behind the others, guarding their back without thinking about it. It'd been a long time since I'd been in a situation like this, but old habits die hard.

ELEVEN

Nox

"Excuse me," I said as I approached the wendigo, my arms loose at my side to appear as unthreatening as I could.

The others were invisible, and they'd surrounded the wendigo at a distance in case he tried to run. I'd been picked as the one to do the talking because I was the least scary of us all. I wasn't sure if I should be happy about that or not, not when I was supposed to be the fearless Keeper of the Chasm.

"Can I help you?" the wendigo asked, his deep brown eyes wary. Despite the inky stains on his soul, I could see how pure it originally was. Was that another *fuck you* from the queen? Intentionally sullying pure souls for the task instead of taking already darkened ones?

"Hey, I'm Nox. There's something I need to tell you, and I know it might seem hard to believe, but please hear me out."

He stared at me contemplatively for a few seconds before nodding. "I'm Dell. My cabin is just around the bend. Would you like to talk there?"

"Sure," I said, knowing the others would follow us. I wasn't in any true danger anyway, since wendigos ate human flesh, and my flesh was very much made up of magic. But I didn't get the mindless monster vibe from this guy, so I didn't think he'd attack me out of the blue.

We'd decided in a hasty discussion as we followed him that we'd tell him everything. If necessary, we could always remove his memories later. It was one of the perks we had as soul collectors, but it wasn't a magic we could use often. Maximus's squad used it the most, since they were responsible for covering up accidental supe sightings.

Once we were in his cabin—which was very sparse but somehow homey at the same time—I took the only chair as he sat on the bed, and I could sense the others crowded around me.

"So, tell me," Dell said as he crossed his arms over his chest, leaning his back against the wall. He was a handsome man, with short blond hair that was longer on the front and deep brown eyes. He had some kind of colorful mark on his chest I could see peeking out his shirt, but it wasn't visible enough to tell what it was. He was slim, almost too thin, and I wondered if he had a habit of starving himself. I'd heard wendigos usually stuck to one of the extremes: starving or gorging. It was clear which side Dell was on.

I took a deep breath and launched into the story. I explained about the witches using dark magic, the potion, and how I suspected he'd been infected. I tried to keep the details as vague as possible, not wanting to reveal more than I had to. Telling the people of the human realm about Otherworld was a big no-no except in special circumstances, and I wanted to avoid doing it if I could. When I'd finished telling him everything, his mouth hung open as he shook his head.

"That makes sense," he murmured after a few minutes of silence, and I froze.

Sitting up straight, I asked, "What makes sense?"

He frowned and rubbed his face, and it was only then that I noticed the dark circles under his eyes. "Since the last couple of weeks, my control has been... slipping. I don't usually need to eat much. A pound or so of... you know... every month is enough. I have a contact who gets me some food, and I'm okay with it. I've learned to control myself. But recently, I've been slipping, losing control. I haven't hurt anybody yet, but I'm so scared it'll happen. I've been avoiding sleep because of it, but today I accidentally fell asleep, and when I came to I was in the middle of an amusement park." He shuddered at the memory, and I couldn't help taking his hand in mine and giving it a squeeze. He blinked down at it as if he wasn't sure what I was doing, and sadness rushed through me at the thought that this man had been so touch-starved that he'd forgotten what a comforting touch felt like.

"We'll help you, okay? We'd like to take you to a safe location where you won't just be protected from the dark souls, but also from your own urges," I assured him, and he nodded slowly.

"Do I need to come with you right away?" he asked, and I shook my head. Maximus had said the safe house wasn't anywhere close to here, and while Harlan could portal Dell there, we'd decided to instead post a few of Maximus's squad members here while we discussed it with Damien.

"No, not yet. We'll leave a few people guarding you. They'll keep anyone unwanted out, and also accompany you anywhere you go and stop you if you start losing control," I assured him, and he slumped back against the wall with a nod.

We exchanged numbers, and I felt magic stir around us but didn't mention it. Once I'd left the cabin and Dell behind, the others reappeared around me, and I turned to Harlan. "What was the magic about?"

"I warded the place against anyone who means Dell harm or has a dark soul. My brief foray into the Chasm was enough for my magic to understand what a black soul is, so now I can ward against it," he explained. That might come in handy later.

"Oh! Could you modify the ward to keep the dark souls inside its limits instead?" I asked, and Harlan's eyes narrowed as he thought over it.

"I think I can. And if I channel Damien's magic, I could make it even stronger," he said, and I made a mental note to mention it to Damien later. With the threat of the queen of Underworld breaking out of the Chasm looming overhead, we needed to put in as many restrictions as we could.

"Okay. Bernard and Felicia will be here in a minute to take up the guard position. Once they're here, we need to get back home and update Damien," Maximus said, and I nodded.

I took Harlan's hand and pulled him a few feet away from the others. Tilting my head up, I met his beautiful blue eyes. "I'm sorry this is how our date ended." I really was bummed. I'd wanted to take him back to my cabin and make out—and maybe more—with him, not...this.

"You have nothing to apologize for, Nox. We just saved someone's life. I'd say it's the perfect way to end our date."

I grinned at that. "Of course you would, my knight. You're all about saving lives, aren't you?"

Before he could answer, I leaned up and pressed my lips to his, sighing as his strong arms instantly wrapped around me. His lips were warm as they covered mine, his tongue teasing as it licked at mine, stealing touches without letting me do the same. Growling into his mouth, I deepened the kiss, nipping at his lips as I delved deeper into his mouth. He moaned roughly, and I considered it a win.

Then something smacked me in the head and I jumped back as a small pebble fell to the ground. I glared at Zane, knowing without doubt it was their doing.

"Time to go home," they called out, waving toward Dell's cabin where Bernie and Fel had already taken their spots.

I looked up at Harlan and he smiled at me as our magic stirred around us and took us home.

Harlan

"We stumbled across him completely by accident, but will we really be able to find the other four before it's too late? What if they're all in different continents?" Nox wondered aloud, but I knew he wasn't the only one thinking the same thing.

"We could drag one of those souls out of the Chasm and question them," Zane suggested, but Damien shook his head.

"Too risky. We don't know what their plan is. Maybe all they need is one person on the outside to break out of there. And anyway, we've tried that before. They won't talk. We had to send Cynthia and the others to the Chasm too since it was getting dangerous holding them here."

Nox had caught me up on everything that had happened until now, and I had to agree. If those dark souls hadn't talked before, they definitely wouldn't talk now that they were so close to the finish line. But there was something niggling at the back of my mind, something Nox had told me. If only I could remember what it was...

"If only there was a way to get the truth from them without getting anyone out of the Chasm," Kym complained, and suddenly, the pieces clicked together.

"That's it!" I said, smacking the table and startling everyone. Smiling sheepishly, I apologized. "Sorry. But what if we could? What if we could ask someone without getting them out of the Chasm?"

"I'd say it's impossible, but I have a feeling I'd be wrong," Zane said, and I smiled.

"I just remembered Nox told me one of the vampires who worked for Cynthia hadn't been sent into the Chasm. That Kym purified his soul until it was no longer dark. What about him?"

"Connor!" Zane hissed, sitting up in their chair. "We can talk to him. He's still in my Redemption center, and considering he really wants to make up for his crimes, I'm sure he'll be happy to help us."

"Perfect. It's getting late, but first thing tomorrow, I want you and Max to talk to Connor. Find out anything you can about the four remaining supes. We also need to figure out a way to heal whatever the potion did to these people."

"Won't my fire work on them?" Kym said, shooting a glare at Maximus that made him snap his mouth shut before he could protest.

"It might. It's something we can try. Why don't you, Nox, and Harlan visit Dell tomorrow and see if you can heal him? Keep your ears and tail hidden and just say you're a healer," Damien said, and Kym nodded, while Nox shot me an excited smile, probably at the prospect of going back to the human realm.

Once the meeting dispersed, Kym, Nox, and I made plans to head to the human realm first thing tomorrow morning, since we didn't want to waste time, especially when poor Dell had to battle his hunger constantly.

"Are you excited about going back to the human realm?" I asked Nox as we stepped into his cabin, and he smiled. We'd only stopped by earlier to get rid of our shirts before going to Damien to update him, and I was glad we had because the Otherworld atmosphere could get really hot.

"A little, yes. I hadn't realized how much I was missing out on until today."

"I bet," I answered with a grin before my smile faltered. "I hope Kym's magic works. And I hope we can take on this queen."

"Me too. I trust Damien and the others. They won't let anything happen to any of us."

"And I won't let anything happen to you," I assured him, and he smiled.

"You're pretty amazing, you know that?" Nox asked as his fingers raked through my beard, and I leaned into the touch.

"People have said that about me once or twice," I answered with a smirk, making him laugh.

Our laughter seamlessly turned into desire as Nox pressed his lips to mine, sparks flying as I pulled him closer to me, our bodies fitting together like they were made for each other. He rocked his groin against my thigh, his erection rubbing against me as he chased the friction. My grip on his jaw tightened as I tilted his head up so I could delve deeper into his addicting mouth.

Nox hefted his leg up, wrapping it around my hip as we continued kissing. Neither of us needed to breathe, so there was nothing to make us pull away from each other. Losing my grip on his jaw, I pulled his other leg around my hip, his arms scrambling to wrap around my neck.

Turning around, I pressed his back to the door, rocking into him so my denim-covered dick rubbed against his ass. His erection was trapped between us, but he didn't seem to mind as I trailed kisses down his jaw, biting at the soft skin of his neck.

He made the sweetest sounds as he moaned against me, and I needed to watch him come. I pulled back, making him whine, his eyes hooded and cheeks flushed as he watched me unbutton both our pants. I pulled his erection out before freeing myself from my pants as well. Spitting in my palm, I wrapped it around both of us and started jacking us before reclaiming his lips.

He moaned into my mouth as I twisted my wrist around us the way I liked doing when I was jerking off, and I gasped as his silky soft skin rubbed against mine. It didn't take long before my climax rushed over me, and I pulled back as I felt Nox shudder, watching as his back arched against the door and he shot all over my chest and abdomen, his mouth open in a wordless scream, his lips red and swollen and his eyes barely open.

I groaned his name as I came, painting his chest with my cum. As aftershocks shuddered through me, I watched with hooded eyes as he dipped his fingers into the cum on his chest—my cum—and sucked them into his mouth. My cock twitched valiantly at the sight, and I shook my head. "Fuck, Nox, you're killing me."

He smirked at me before leaning over to kiss me, and I groaned as I tasted myself on him. Fuck, he was addictive.

"Come on, we need a shower," I murmured against his lips, and he smiled.

"All right."

Once we were under the shower, holding each other close and not doing much to actually clean ourselves, Nox looked up at me, his eyes warm and molten silver. "Thank you for today. I had a lot of fun."

I smiled as I tucked his wet hair behind his ears, tapping his nose before pulling away. "I had fun too. It was a great day."

"It truly was. I don't think I've ever had that much fun." His smile fell suddenly, and he slapped his forehead. "Shoot! I forgot to talk to Damien about finding a second Keeper."

"There's no hurry. We can ask tomorrow after we come back from the human realm," I said, and his smile returned.

"You're right. I just want to get it out of the way before I get back into the work routine, you know? I'm worried I'll get too caught up in it if I do, and I won't want to let go."

"If that happens, I'll forcibly pull you away from it if that's what it takes. How does that sound?"

He grinned widely and hopped onto his toes to smack a kiss on my lips. "It sounds perfect."

TWELVE

Nox

"So, Kym, you ready to do this?" I asked, throwing my arm around his shoulders. Max narrowed his eyes at me, but I ignored him.

"Yep. Is it weird that this is the first time I'm going to the human realm without Max?" he asked, and I shook my head.

"Not at all. You haven't been here that long, so it makes sense. Harlan, you ready?"

"When you are," he answered, and I took his hand. Maximus waved at his mate and I let my magic lead us to the cabin we'd left Dell at. Maximus had decided that until we found the others, it'd be easier to keep Dell safe at his own cabin.

"Hey, Fel, hey, Bernie. We'll be here for a bit, so you should go home and send your reliefs. You've been here long enough."

"Sure thing, Nox. It's been quiet all night," Bernie said, and I nodded.

The two disappeared back to Otherworld and I headed to the front door, knocking softly. "Dell? It's Nox from yesterday."

The door opened, and Dell blinked out at me, his eyes bloodshot and his hair all over the place.

"Uh, you okay, man?" I asked. He didn't look so good.

"I'm fine. Come on in."

I led the way, Harlan and Kym trailing behind me as I introduced them. "Dell, this is my mate, Harlan. And this is Kym. He's a healer, and we hoped he might be able to heal you."

Dell blinked at Kym, hope sparking in his eyes. Kym had used magic to hide his fox tail and ears, so he looked human for all intents and purposes, though as a supe Dell could probably sense Kym wasn't quite human.

"That would be wonderful," he murmured. He led us to the bed since there was only one chair, and we settled on it as he took the chair. Something clinked against the side of the bed, and I peeked over to find a handcuff hanging over the side. I raised a brow at him, and he flushed. "I didn't want to accidentally go on a hunt again. I mean, I trust your people, but I couldn't sleep..." He trailed off, and Kym leaned forward, placing a palm on his hand.

"It's okay. I can't imagine what you must be feeling like. I really hope I can help you."

Dell blinked at him, then me, and then Harlan. His eyes came back to me as he said, "You guys are different."

I froze. Had he somehow guessed we weren't from the human realm? "Different how?" I asked, struggling to keep my voice nonchalant.

"Well, the moment someone finds out what I am, they run the other way. They don't offer to help me." Then, in a much softer voice that I was sure we weren't supposed to hear, he added, "They definitely never touch me."

My heart hurt for this man. Loneliness seemed to seep out of him, and I hated that he was living a life of seclusion because of people who had made him feel so unaccepted.

"Come on, let's try this. Kym, do you need anything from us?" I asked, and Kym shook his head.

To Dell, he said, "Can I take your other hand?"

Dell nodded, and Kym gripped both his hands, bowing his head over them as he closed his eyes and focused. White light shone between their palms, and Dell bit his lip, a shiver racing through him.

I shared a look with Harlan, and he took my hand in his, giving it a light squeeze.

"I can feel the damage. I think I can burn it, but it'll take a lot of energy. Max won't like it," Kym muttered, and Harlan raised a brow at me.

"He burned himself out when he purified Connor, and Max wasn't happy, to put it lightly," I explained, and Harlan nodded in a way that told me he agreed with Maximus. What was it with these big, muscly mates who thought we weren't capable of taking care of ourselves?

I mean, sure, I'd jumped into the Chasm without a backup plan, and sure, I'd almost died... huh. Maybe it wasn't so bad that they were looking out for us. Maybe we actually needed that.

Shaking my head at my wayward thoughts, I focused back on the duo locked in magic. Harlan placed a palm on Kym's shoulder and shook him. "Kym, stop. You'll burn yourself out. Maybe you should try channeling me."

Kym sat up slowly, blinking a few times before looking at Harlan. "I've never done that before. How do I channel you?"

"Nox, can you find a knife, please?" Harlan asked, and I leaned forward and pulled the one in my boots out. It was a small knife Zane had gifted me last year, and they'd taught me how to throw it hard enough that it'd be in and out of someone's heart before they noticed.

Harlan looked surprised I'd had a knife on me, and I chuckled as I handed it over. He pricked his skin with the knife and asked Kym for his hand, doing the same to him. Then he pressed their bloodied fingers together and murmured a spell I couldn't make out.

"Okay, I've opened my magic to you. Now all you have to do is draw it toward you and then use it to power your ability," Harlan said, and Kym nodded slowly.

Focusing back on Dell, Kym closed his eyes, his jaw clenched as he worked his magic. If I focused on Dell's soul, I could see Kym's magic at work. The black marks on Dell's soul were blazing at the corners, growing smaller in size little by little.

Harlan blew out a breath beside me, and I turned to him. His back was rigid, his free hand curled in a fist. I didn't need to be a warlock to know he was giving up more magic than he should. I guess I wasn't the only one without self-preservation in this couple.

Dell's soul looked much better than it had before. Unfortunately, it still wasn't completely healed. But that didn't mean I'd let Harlan and Kym burn out.

"Stop," I said, my voice low but firm. "You're both nearing burnout, and we don't need that when we still have four others to help. Let's take a break to replenish your energy, and then we'll get back to it. Dell, how are you feeling?"

Dell blinked his eyes open, and they were full of unshed tears. A single drop slid down his cheek, and he quickly wiped it away. He'd clearly been in pain, but he hadn't made a sound. I didn't know what to think about that.

"I feel better. More in control. Thank you," he murmured, and Kym squeezed his hand.

"My pleasure. We'll be back later to finish the job, okay? Please stay here until then. Would you like us to get you some food?"

His face went white, and Dell shook his head quickly. I wondered what his story was, how he'd come to be a wendigo. I had a feeling it wasn't a pretty story. Then again, stories about the creation of a human-eating monster rarely were.

We left soon after, promising to be back later that evening to finish healing him. The two soul collectors who'd replaced Bernie and Fel stood guard at the cabin as we returned to Otherworld, and I hoped Maximus and Zane had been as successful in their task as we had.

Harlan

"He had no inkling where the other three could be?" I asked, and Zane shook their head.

"According to Connor, only Cynthia knew the location of all five. She gave each of her most trusted minions one potion and one name. Connor told us the one he was in charge of. We still need to find the other three, but the only one who knows their whereabouts is Cynthia."

"But we'd need to bring her out of the Chasm if we want to talk to her. Maybe we shouldn't have sent her into the Chasm," Maximus said with a frown.

"Keeping them out was starting to get dangerous. We made the right call," Nox argued, and Max nodded, though it was clear he wasn't happy about it.

Remembering something or rather someone who might be able to help, I said, "I know someone who might be able to talk to the witch without removing her from the Chasm. I've never seen him in action, but I've heard he's quite powerful. He's a necromancer," I explained, and everyone started talking over each other, mostly about how unworthy of trust necromancers were.

"We can trust him. He's part of the Mistvale clan. The same clan that adopted those kids last year. The same clan I belonged to in my previous life," I added.

The murmurs cut off abruptly as Maximus made a thoughtful sound. To me, he said, "I trust Raiden's clan. They've helped us before. We can't send you, though. They can't know about Otherworld, so they can't know about you. You understand, don't you?"

I blinked. I actually hadn't thought about getting to go back. I'd mostly been focused on finding a solution. But now that Maximus had mentioned it, I wished I could go. I wanted to see how my family, my clan was doing.

"We could go as invisible backup. The way you were with me when I talked to Dell," Nox piped up, even though we both knew they wouldn't need backup for something like this.

I didn't know if Maximus felt sorry for me or if he was just that much of a good guy, but he agreed with Nox. "I'll go to talk to them, since they already know me. Nox and Harlan can be my backup. I'll need to make sure they don't find out more than they need to. And if they do, I might have to make them forget. They're very good allies to us, but we can't break our rules for anyone."

"Lionel and Mazia can find the supe Connor told us about," Zane said, and Max nodded.

"I'm going to go update Damien about everything. Then we can head to Mistvale. The sooner we find the other three supes, the better."

Once Maximus left to talk to Damien and Zane went in search of their mate, Nox dragged me back to the cabin, saying Max would call us when it was time to go.

"Are you okay?" Nox asked as we stepped into the cabin, and I smiled at him.

"Of course. Just a little nervous about going to Mistvale. I know they won't see me, and I can't talk to them, but I really want to see how they're doing. My sister, my best friend, and I spent decades together, only depending on each other. I was the caretaker of the trio, and I would've been more worried if they hadn't both found their mates before my death." I made a face and shook my head. "It's so weird to think about my death. It doesn't feel real."

Nox smiled softly, pressing himself to me as he tilted his head up to meet my eyes. "I know it doesn't. That's why we call this our second life. *Death* is just what the ones in the human realm call it. To us, it's just a transition. Or you could call it rebirth."

"Rebirth. I like that."

"Now, can I interest you in a makeout session until Maximus calls?" Nox asked with a slight smirk, and I grinned as I tipped his chin up, claiming his lips with mine.

THIRTEEN

Nox

I watched as Raiden, the dragon who headed the Mistvale clan, and whose house we were in, talked to Maximus, completely oblivious to our presence. It felt weird to be invisible. It'd been a long fucking time since I'd been this unnoticeable.

"Man, I can walk up to that dragon and lick his face, and he wouldn't even notice," I mused, and Harlan raised a brow at me.

"Do you usually go around licking strange men, mate?" he asked, and I grinned.

"Nah, not really. Uh, but I should tell you, Zane and I had a thing going until they found their mate." I'd been thinking of telling him for a while now, but maybe I should've waited until we were in my cabin to say something. I didn't know how Harlan would react.

Whatever I'd thought he'd do at the revelation, tilting his head and saying, "That makes sense," wasn't it.

"It does?" I asked skeptically, and he nodded.

"I could see from the start you and Zane have a special bond. I thought it was just friendship, but now I understand it better."

"We're not in love or anything," I clarified hurriedly because that's what his words had sounded like. "Zane loves Wren, and I... Well, I have you now." *And someday soon, I'll love you just like that.*

"I understand that. Don't worry. No one can see Zane and Wren together and not realize how in love they are. I just meant you have a stronger connection with Zane than possibly anyone else in your family," Harlan clarified, and I hummed thoughtfully. I was close to a lot of people in my family, but if I had to pick the one I was closest to, it'd be Zane without a doubt.

"You're right. Zane is pretty special to me, but our sexual relationship is in the past now." I didn't want there to be any doubts about that.

"I trust you, Nox."

I smiled at him before tuning back into the conversation between Raiden and Maximus. Max had felt it'd be better to talk to Raiden instead of approaching the necromancer directly, and Harlan had agreed that it'd be the better move, so here we were.

"I can't tell you a lot, but we need Aeron's help to find out some pertinent information from a witch who died a few weeks ago," Maximus was saying, and I wondered if it was selfish of me to be thankful that the witch had *killed* Harlan before she died. It was wrong, wasn't it? But I'd waited so long for Harlan, and I couldn't help being happy about his death, even though he'd been ripped away from his family. I could've waited another few decades, sure, but it'd have been awful.

I shook my head, pushing away the thoughts and focusing on the conversation at hand instead.

Raiden was an attractive dragon, with stunning platinum hair, gray eyes that seemed to change colors, and a lean build that made him appear taller than Maximus even though he wasn't. Max had said he was quite old, but like most supes, his age didn't show on his face at all. He looked like he was in his late twenties at the most.

"Aeron is at work right now, but I can have him here in fifteen minutes. Is it okay if his mate accompanies him?" Raiden asked, and I winced. More people meant more memories to alter, and that wasn't good.

"He can come with, but I'd like to work with Aeron alone. The less people who know the details, the better."

Raiden thought over it a beat and then nodded. "Can we meet at the pack land in half an hour? The meeting room there is soundproofed and it has enough room for Aeron to work in."

"Sounds good. I can also check in with the kids before I leave," Maximus agreed, and I smiled at the big softie. I'd only recently found out he still visited the kids he'd rescued with Wren, and it made me wonder if maybe our fearless leader had a fatherly side we knew nothing about. He wasn't close to Walker, but that was only because Walker had found him intimidating for a while before letting his guard down around him.

I followed Max and Harlan, half lost in thought, as we left Raiden's house. Apparently, he was a stay-at-home dad for the most part, so we'd had to visit him at home. It was probably why he'd asked to reconvene at the pack's place. No man would want an evil witch summoned at his home.

Once we were in the hotel room Max had booked to *keep up appearances*—which had seemed over the top to me at first but made sense when an overprotective rich as fuck dragon was involved—Harlan and I turned ourselves visible and I leaped onto the bed, grinning as I bounced.

"I love this mattress," I declared. Maximus rolled his eyes, but Harlan winked at me before jumping onto the mattress and making me bounce again. Except I'd misjudged how close to the edge I was, and I tumbled off the side as I landed, crashing onto the wood floor.

"Fuck, Nox! You okay?" Harlan asked as he leaned over the side, and I smiled.

"I'm fine, I'm fine. Mortal things can't hurt us, remember? We could've leapt over the roller coaster when it was at its highest, and we wouldn't have had a scratch to show for it." My eyes lit up as an idea struck, and I sat up, grabbing Harlan's hand.

Before I could share my masterful idea with him, he cut me off. "No, we're not leaping off a running rollercoaster."

"Aww man," I groaned, giving him a pout. "But it'd be so fun!"

"I don't like heights," Harlan admitted, and I scowled at him.

"Bullshit. You were on all the rides with me."

"With my eyes shut and a stream of *oh shit*s running through my head. I know it's stupid to be afraid of heights when I can't die, but I can't turn it off."

Realizing he was serious, I climbed off the floor and joined him on the bed, taking his hand in mine. "It's not stupid. I'm sorry I pushed you."

"You didn't," he assured me before kissing me, softly at first before going deeper.

It was just about to turn from intense to need-you-out-of-your-clothes hot when someone cleared their throat, and we jerked apart.

"Shall I leave you two to it?" Max asked with a smirk, and I threw a pillow at him. He'd just cost me a sexy romp with my mate; he was lucky I'd thrown the pillow and not the lamp.

Max ducked the pillow with a chuckle before straightening up and stretching his arms over his head. "I'm going to go sit in the lobby downstairs. You have fifteen minutes."

Fifteen minutes, huh? I could do a lot in fifteen minutes.

Harlan

After the best blowjob of my life, it took me a few minutes to float back to the present. Realizing our fifteen minutes were almost up, we cleaned up quickly. Just as we were getting done, there was a knock at the door.

Nox let Maximus in as I ran my fingers through my hair to get back into some semblance of order. The smirk on Maximus's face said he knew exactly what we'd been up to, and I felt my cheeks burn. I wasn't a prude or anything, but Nox wasn't just a hook-up. He was my mate, and I wanted to keep our private time private. Was that too much to hope for?

Considering how involved the Otherworlders were in each others' lives, I had to say yes. But I didn't mind it too much because it reminded me of the Mistvalers and the family I'd left behind.

Now that it was time, I was eager to see them again, even if I wouldn't get to actually talk to any of them. I wanted to see my sister, to make sure she was happy. I wanted to see how much my niece and nephew had grown. It hadn't been that long since I'd been gone, but still.

"You ready?" Nox asked softly, taking my hand in his and looking up at me with his steel-gray eyes.

I nodded, and we turned ourselves invisible again as we followed Maximus out of the room. He'd rented a car to avoid suspicion too, and we piled in. The drive to the pack land was short, but I spent it all taking in the familiar surroundings and telling Nox snippets about my time there. I hadn't lived in Mistvale that long, but it was still the place that had felt most like home until I came to Otherworld. Now, that was my home. Nox was my home.

"You miss this place, don't you?" Nox asked, his voice warm.

I shrugged, turning my attention to him. "I do. I mean, don't get me wrong. I love being in Otherworld. I love being with you. But after spending years looking for a home, Mistvale was the first place that felt like it could be it, you know? Not to mention my sister and best friend live here."

"I understand. Once upon a time, I had family in the human realm too. They're long gone now, probably living another life already, but I remember wishing I could see them once more, talk to them."

I pressed a kiss to his temple because it was the only thing I could think of, and he smiled an almost shy smile. Before he could say anything, the car came to a stop, and I looked up to realize we were in the pack land already.

Nox had to nudge me to get me moving because now that we were here, it'd finally sunk in that I was really going to see Rhiannon and my niece and nephew.

Raiden was waiting for us with Rebba—the alpha of the Mistvale pack and Rhiannon's mate—and Rhiannon, their babies cradled in their arms, both sleeping peacefully. I wished I could hold them, but I was fine just knowing they were safe and healthy.

Rhiannon shifted the baby in her arms, and my eyes fell on the pendant hanging on a chain around her neck. The blue was the color of our eyes, and realizing what it was was a shock I hadn't been prepared for.

I knew I was dead. I'd thought I'd accepted that fact. But seeing my warlock stone—something that was formed from the ashes of a dead warlock so they could pass their magic and blessings to their successors—around my sister's neck was a stark reminder that struck me harder than I'd expected it to.

Despite myself, I leaned forward and brushed my fingers over the stone. In this form, I couldn't actually touch the stone. My fingers passed right through it, but something in it must've recognized me because it glowed faintly, and judging by Rhiannon's gasp, she'd seen it too.

She looked around, as if expecting to see me, and I couldn't help but smile. I brushed my fingers over her cheek, not feeling anything but a slight warmth. She didn't react, but the way Rebba leaned over to ask if she was okay assured me she was in good hands. Rebba was a great alpha, and an even better mate. My sister would be well taken care of.

While I'd been caught up in Rhiannon, Maximus and Raiden had been joined by two more people. I hadn't spent a lot of time with Aeron and Niall when I was alive, but they were a part of the clan, which meant they were good people. While Aeron was a necromancer, Niall was a vampire. They were an unlikely pair since necromancers were known for their ability to control the undead, but it was clear they loved each other. The gecko sitting on Niall's shoulder made me smile. Blizzard was Aeron's familiar, but every time I'd seen them, I'd found him on Niall.

"I promise you Aeron will not come to any harm," Maximus said, a palm on his chest as if he was swearing an oath.

Niall met Aeron's eyes, and they seemed to have some kind of wordless communication. In the end, Niall slumped and blew out a breath. "Fine. But if he even gets so much as a scratch..."

"I won't let anything happen to Aeron," Raiden assured him, his voice warm and firm.

Niall nodded mutely, trusting Raiden more than he'd trust Maximus, which made sense. I knew very well how powerful Raiden was, and I wasn't confident Maximus could take him if it came down to it.

"All right, then. Let's summon a witch."

FOURTEEN

Nox

While I trusted Maximus and Harlan's judgment, I hadn't been a hundred percent sure about asking a necromancer for help. As the Keeper, I'd dealt with necromancers who didn't understand their limits and couldn't pull back after channeling a soul. I'd stepped in more than once to drag a soul back to the Chasm.

But Aeron was different. His soul was free of too many blemishes, and he was careful in the way he set up for the channeling. He didn't need to draw a circle since he wouldn't be summoning all of Cynthia, just enough of her consciousness so she'd be able to answer our questions. Or at least, that was how he'd explained things to Maximus as he settled cross-legged on the meeting room floor.

"I need a name and something that belongs to the person. It'll make it easier to make a connection," Aeron said, and Maximus pulled something out of his pocket and handed it over, as if he'd expected it.

It was a knife, I realized. *Cynthia's* knife. Where, when, and how had he acquired it?

"The name is Cynthia," he said, and Aeron took the knife, holding it in both hands as he closed his eyes.

I glanced over at Harlan, whose eyes were on Raiden. He'd insisted on joining, not just because of his promise to Niall, but because Aeron might need a power boost and he was the best source. Raiden's brows were furrowed, and he looked deep in thought.

"What is it?" I asked Harlan, keeping my voice low even though there was no way the dragon would be able to hear us.

"I don't know. I think Raiden's getting suspicious. He reacted at the name. Do you think he made the connection?"

"Did he know the name of your killer?" I asked, and Harlan narrowed his eyes.

"I don't remember. Everything happened so fast that night."

"It's okay. Maximus will handle it. Trust him."

"She's here," Aeron announced even though we could clearly see her, which told me supes couldn't see the souls Aeron summoned.

Cynthia's soul was fainter since she wasn't fully here, but the sickly aura of black magic still clung to her.

"Ooh, a necromancer! What I wouldn't give for a taste of your magic." She almost purred the words, and Aeron's face screwed up in disgust.

"What did she say?" Maximus asked, acting like he couldn't hear her. Of course. Keeping up our cover was as important as finding the information we needed.

"Nothing worth repeating. What do you want me to ask?"

"Ask her where the other three infected supes are," Maximus said, and Raiden sucked in a breath, his eyes flashing. His fists were curled tight, and I could almost feel his anger. He reminded me of Damien, of the way he was so quick to anger on behalf of any of us.

The sky rumbled outside, Raiden's emotions slipping out into the Mistvale weather. It had to be tough being a storm dragon and displaying all your emotions across the sky.

Aeron didn't react, merely making eye contact with Cynthia as he demanded, "Where are the other three supes you infected, Cynthia?"

"I didn't infect anyone," she replied, clearly not intending to make this easy for us. Necromancers had the ability to demand truth, but they still needed to ask the right questions.

"Where are the supes you ordered to be infected?" Aeron demanded, still with that calm voice.

"I have no idea. I didn't exactly leash them, you know?"

Ugh, I was growing really tired of this bitch. I took a step forward with no idea what I'd do, but Harlan grabbed me before I could take more than a couple of steps.

"You can't do anything to her here, remember?" he reminded me softly, and I blew out a breath as I stepped into him, letting him wrap an arm around my waist.

"Sorry. She got on my nerves."

"Trust me, you're not alone. But we need to let Aeron handle this."

"Where were the supes when you had them infected?" Aeron asked, and this time there was a strain in his voice. Raiden must've heard it too because he stepped closer, placing a palm on Aeron's shoulder. He must've channeled his magic into him. Aeron sat up, his shoulders straightening with the burst of power. Looked like the dragon didn't need to use a spell to lend his magic.

"One was in Chicago, another in London. And one in...hmm...oh yeah, Nevada. Though who knows where they are now. I'm guessing you found the wendigo. And you got Connor to turn. That vampire was always a little too squeamish," Cynthia drawled, looking for all the world like she couldn't care less.

Aeron repeated the words for Max's benefit, and his brows furrowed, consternation clear on his face. "Ask her what the infected supes are. We need a narrower pool."

Aeron repeated the question, and she evaded his attempts until he'd rephrased his question for the fourth time. "One is a kelpie, one a fae away from home, and one a wyvern."

"A wyvern? I thought they were extinct," Harlan murmured, and I shook my head.

"They've just abandoned humanity in favor of the wild. They live in the mountains, in risky-as-fuck places where humans wouldn't dare venture."

"Damn," Harlan murmured, sounding awed, and I decided I'd take him to visit the wyverns soon. Maybe we could take Kym there since I doubted the wyvern would be willing to come anywhere close to civilization.

"I can't hold on much longer. Any more questions?" My respect for Aeron grew. He clearly knew his limits, and I respected that. It was something I had a problem with myself, as shown by my recent adventure.

"I don't think so. You can let her go," Maximus said, and Aeron relaxed.

"Hope you can figure out which supe is at which location in time!" Cynthia called just before she disappeared, and I growled. That bitch!

Aeron relayed what she'd said just like he'd been relaying each reply, not knowing we could see and hear her just fine, and Maximus swore under his breath.

Shaking his head, he shook Aeron's hand once he was standing. "Thank you so much for your help."

"No worries. If that's all, I'm going to go check on Niall."

Raiden waited until Aeron was out of the room before turning to Max. "Now, will you tell me why you needed answers from the woman who killed a member of my clan and hurt another?"

Well, it looked like Raiden had made the connection after all.

Harlan

I should've expected that. When I'd suggested getting Aeron's help, I should've realized there was a chance one of them would make a connection between the witch who killed me and the one we were talking to. Raiden was old, experienced, and smart. How had I ever thought we'd be able to get past him?

I eyed Maximus, worried how he'd tackle this. He looked deep in thought before he nodded to himself and met Raiden's eyes. "I can't tell you everything, please understand that. Cynthia is part of a much bigger group we're trying to get our hands on. They've been playing with dark magic in a way no one should be allowed to. We're doing everything we can to track them down before they do any more damage to this world and the people in it."

Well...none of what he'd said was a lie. It was actually pretty smart, the way he'd evaded giving any concrete facts and still said enough to appease Raiden.

Raiden looked thoughtful as he mulled over what he'd said. "And what about the infected supes? Who are they?"

Maximus sighed, anger and concern clashing in his dark eyes. "Results of an experiment gone wrong. They used dark magic on some supes to try to alter their makeup. Lord knows what their endgame was, but now the supes are out there, suffering the consequences with no idea what's wrong with them. We've tracked down two, and now we'll hopefully find the other three. Luckily, we have someone who can heal them."

"And I suppose asking who 'we' is would be a futile endeavor?" Raiden asked with a raised brow, and Maximus smiled.

"Sorry, I can't tell you. It's for everyone's best. But I assure you we'll take care of this."

"I don't doubt it. If any of the supes need a safe space, please know Mistvale will always welcome them."

This. This was why Mistvale had felt like home. Because the dragon who looked over it was a warmhearted being who would never turn away someone in need. After what I'd done to Oliver—one of the shifters in Raiden's clan—I hadn't expected forgiveness, much less an invite to join their clan. Yet that was what I'd gotten, and I couldn't be more thankful I'd accepted, even if I'd only gotten to stay with them for a short time.

"I'll keep that in mind. On that note, I was hoping to see the kids before I left. I promised I'd check in with them, and with the way things are going, I might not be able to see them for a while after this."

"Of course. They're all probably studying right now. Firey and Noel have taken to teaching them in the woods. They say it's less restricting," Raiden explained with a shrug, and I smiled. My best friend was a teacher now, huh? I could imagine that. Firey was warm and nurturing, exactly what these kids needed. And Noel had earned the title of pack mama, so who better to take care of a bunch of kids?

"Lead the way, then," Maximus said, and Raiden started to head toward the door before stopping.

"One last thing. Jules's captivity, and then the kids', the attacks on Jules...they're all related, aren't they? To this group that uses dark magic?"

Maximus took a beat to answer, probably deciding if it was something that would create more questions than he could answer. In the end, he nodded. "They are, yes. We've been hunting them for a while, but we're closing in now, I assure you."

Raiden nodded. "Let me know if you need any help. We're not fighters, but we can offer sanctuary to anyone in need."

Maximus smiled and placed his palm on Raiden's upper arm, squeezing lightly. "I don't doubt that. Bringing those kids here was one of the best decisions I made. You've created a beautiful community here, and any supe would be lucky to be a part of it."

Raiden seemed pleased with the compliment, which he should be. He'd earned it.

"You know, we might have to come back here soon. I want to explore this town now. I want to see your favorite spots. Will you show me?" I glanced down at Nox, who was watching me with warm gray eyes, a slight smile on his lips. I leaned down and pressed a chaste kiss to them, unable to resist temptation.

"I'd love to. For now, let me pseudo-introduce you to my best friend."

He chuckled as he slid his arm into the crook of my elbow, and we followed Maximus and Raiden out of the meeting room. A wolf peeked out of the bushes at us, and I smiled. I loved how open everyone was around here. No fear of getting spotted by humans.

"That's Caleb," I said, nodding toward the wolf whose eyes tracked Maximus. "He's Noel's mate, who you'll meet in a bit."

"He looks intense," Nox commented, and I chuckled. He wasn't wrong, but after you'd seen a wolf chasing two tweens with glitter soaking his fur, he stopped being all that scary.

"Kids! You have a visitor!" Raiden called out as we stepped into a clearing, and all the chatter stopped as the kids turned to look at Maximus. My eyes were on my best friend, though, and the soft smile on his face. He looked happy.

My heart warmed with contentment, something peaceful settling in my chest now that I knew for sure everyone I cared about was doing well. The sight of my warlock stone at the base of his throat had me swallowing back tears. I'd always known our bond was unbreakable, but seeing the proof around his neck hit me harder than I'd expected it to.

"You okay?" Nox asked, his palm a comforting weight against my back.

"Yeah. Just glad everyone I love here is happy," I admitted, and Nox smiled, giving me a side-hug as we watched the youngest of the kids, a six-year-old named Dean, chatter on at Maximus, who seemed to be listening to him with utter fascination.

"After this, do you want to go on a date?" Nox asked, and I turned to him.

"What did you have in mind?"

"A surprise," he answered with a cheeky grin, and I shook my head.

"I'd love to go on a date with you."

"Get ready for the best date of your life, then."

FIFTEEN

Nox

I scratched the back of my head as I paced, annoyed at myself for the declaration I'd made.

Best date of his life? Seriously? When I couldn't even remember if I'd *ever* taken anyone on a date.

Harlan was off with Maximus to update Damien about everything we'd learned, and I'd told them I needed to make arrangements for our date. As if I had it all planned.

Maybe I should ask someone for help. Most of my family would probably be just as clueless as me, but there were a few people who could help.

Like Reece and Artemus.

Decision made, I used my magic to get to the Brume Villa, even though my cabin wasn't all that far away. Damien had asked me to move to the villa while I was taking a break from the Burning Chasm, but I'd declined since the cabin was my home, and I felt more comfortable there. Not that the Villa wasn't comfy as fuck. All my family lived there, and while they could be a bit much sometimes, I still loved them with my whole heart.

I knocked on the door of the suite on the third floor that belonged to Damien and his family and tapped my foot against the floor as I waited for someone to open it. The only other living space on this floor was Caelan's suite, which was closed up at the moment since he wasn't here. I imagined once he was back—which probably wouldn't happen for another dozen or so years—Walker would move into the apartment with him, leaving this one for his dads. There was still time for that, sure, but when you've lived as long as I have, twelve years don't seem all that long.

"Nox, come on in! How are you doing?" Artemus said as he opened the door wider, and I gave him a short bow before stepping in.

"I'm perfect, as always."

A smack to the back of my head made me jump, and I rubbed the spot as I glared at Arty. "That hurt." It hadn't, actually, but no one ever said I didn't know how to be dramatic.

"Good. I hoped it would. That was for the absolutely moronic thing you did."

"I got the information we needed," I challenged, and he stepped closer to me, his eyes narrowing.

"And if your mate hadn't found you in time, we could've lost you. No amount of information is worth losing you, you got that?"

I bit my lip as warmth spread through my chest. I knew my family cared about me—of course I did. But knowing something and experiencing it were two completely different things.

Before I did something embarrassing like tear up and start bawling, I threw myself at Arty, hugging him tightly. "I'm sorry. I won't do anything like that ever again."

"You better not. And if you need us to find a new Keeper, you let me know, okay? You have Harlan now, and we'd all understand if you wanted to be free of the Chasm."

"I don't—" I started protesting, unable to imagine anyone doing the job I'd been doing for the past few centuries, even though that was exactly what I'd intended to suggest myself. Was I hesitating because I loved my job that much? Or because I didn't want everything to change?

Arty pulled back, cutting me off with a shake of his head. "Think about it while you're on your break, and we'll discuss it later. Now, what brought you here?"

I blinked as I cleared my head enough to remember why I'd come to him in the first place. When I did, my eyes widened, and I flapped my hands. "Oh shit. I need your help. It's urgent. I can't believe I forgot!"

"Nox, calm down. Tell me what you need help with. Slowly."

I rolled my eyes but did as he'd said. "I want to take Harlan on a date. Actually, I promised him I'd take him on the best date of his life."

"And?" Arty asked when I didn't continue and I glared at him.

"And I have no idea how to do that because I can't even remember if I ever took anyone on a date! Help me! Please?" I grabbed his hands and squeezed tightly, deciding I wouldn't let go until he agreed.

"How about dinner at a fancy restaurant?" Reece called out, and a moment later, he and Walker stepped out of Walker's room. The little one hurried over to me, his hazel eyes wide as he clutched my free hand.

"Is it true, Nox? Is Harlan your mate?"

I couldn't help grinning, both at his earnestness and the fact that Harlan *was* my mate.

"It sure is. Have you met him?"

He nodded as Ro'Shassz uncurled from around his neck—his preferred spot these days—and slithered off to who knew where. Probably a quieter place to sleep in.

"I did. He took care of you when you got hurt. He's nice."

Considering how long it took Walker to warm up to most people, I was ecstatic that Harlan had already earned his approval.

Seemingly done with the conversation, he turned to Reece. "Can I go play with Kitty?"

Reece and Arty had one of their silent conversations, but I understood their reluctance, since Kitty a.k.a. Caelan had a good reason to keep a distance from Walker while he was so young. But whether it was because of their bond, or because Walker was just fond of cats, he'd grown an attachment to Caelan that no one could ignore, and no one wanted to force Walker to stay away from Caelan when playing with him made him so happy.

"Please? I won't stay long, I promise. I don't want to bother him too much." His voice turned small at the end, and Reece shook his head, smiling down at him.

"You'd never be a bother to him, sweetie. Go on ahead. I think I saw him in the lounge a little while ago."

Walker smiled widely and hurried out of the room, and Reece sighed. "It's such a fine line to walk. If we didn't know Caelan as well as we do, I'd never let them spend time together."

"Caelan would never do anything he shouldn't," I said, and Arty patted my arm.

"We know. Doesn't mean we don't still worry, especially since everyone but Vaishnavi's team has been so disconnected from children. Anyway, why don't you let go of my hand and come take a seat. Let's brainstorm a date that will sweep Harlan off his feet."

I grinned as I dropped his hand. I hadn't even realized I'd still been holding on to it. I followed them to the sitting area, sure that between the three of us, we'd figure out an awesome date plan. We had to. After all, I'd promised Harlan the best date of his life.

Harlan

"Wear something comfortable," Nox directed, and I glanced down at the faded jeans I wore. It had taken me a while to get used to the no-shirt attire of Otherworld, but it was a necessity with the heat.

Still, everyone had a few shirts they threw on when they needed to visit the human realm in their visible form for some reason. I pulled on a pale blue shirt and raised a brow at Nox. "This okay?"

His gaze roamed over me, and the intensity of it made me feel as if his fingers were caressing me. I let him get his fill, swallowing hard when his heated gaze met mine. "You look perfect." He shook his head, as if shaking off the lust, and offered me his hand. "Come on, it's date time."

"The best date of my life, right?" I asked with a smile, and he smirked, though there was the slightest hint of nerves in his eyes. Before I could assure him any date with him would be the best one of my life, he was speaking.

"Right. Here we go."

Magic stirred around us, and then we were in a...park. I looked around, brows rising as I realized the place looked familiar.

"Are we...are we in Silent Creek park? In Mistvale?" I asked as I turned to Nox, and he squeezed my hand, giving me an unsure look as he nodded.

"I made sure there was no one around, I promise. And we're invisible, so no one will spot us even if they do come around. I thought you might like to spend some time here."

His rambling was cute, but it showed me how nervous he was about this, and I couldn't have that, so I placed a palm on his cheek, pressing my thumb on his lips to keep him from continuing.

"Shhh...I get it. And I love that you thought about this. This is definitely the best date of my life, mostly because I get to spend it with you."

Nox made a gagging sound, but the twinkle in his eyes told me he secretly liked my sappy side. Well, good, because he was the only reason I had it in the first place.

"We can't exactly have a picnic, but I thought we could sit and talk. Get to know each other a little better. With everything going on, who knows if we'll get another chance like this?"

I sighed, knowing he was right. I wished we'd met under better circumstances, but I knew there was a reason everything had happened when it did. If I'd died a few minutes later or earlier, Zane and I might not have been where we were at the right moment to spot Nox entering the Chasm. We could've ended up being too late to save him, and I'd have never discovered he was my mate until I myself went to Afterworld.

No, everything had happened exactly when it should have, and now all we could do was make the most of the time we had.

I followed Nox to a clearing, breathing in the scent of pine and grass and Mistvale. It felt good to be here, to breathe the same air as my family even if that was all I could share with them.

I shook my head, pushing the past where it belonged. Nox was my present and my future, and he was the one I needed to focus on now.

Nox pretty much skipped over to the base of a huge tree, full of energy that he never seemed to be without. Even when he'd been bedridden, he'd been buzzing with it.

The tree he led me to had branches arching out in every direction, its base surrounded by grass and wildflowers. He settled with his back to the trunk before tugging me toward him until I was seated beside him.

"Put your head in my lap," he directed, and I raised a brow at him but complied, laying down in the slightly wet grass and resting my head on his thigh.

His fingers immediately sank into my hair, running through the short strands in a repetitive motion that threatened to put me to sleep.

To avoid that outcome, I looked up into his eyes, the gray looking almost silver as he smiled down at me. The white strand in his otherwise brown hair hung forward, and I raised a hand to tug at it. "How did you get this? Or is it dyed?"

He shook his head. "It's natural. It just sort of happened. Not all at once, but the hair started graying after I'd been the Keeper for a few decades, and before I knew it, I had a whole strand of white hair that just wouldn't go away. I even chopped it off once, and it grew back white. So I gave up and just decided to call it a fashion statement."

I chuckled at that, not finding it hard to imagine him doing something like that. "How long have you been the Keeper? Can I ask that?"

His eyes turned serious for a moment, his fingers pushing the hair back from my forehead as he said, "You can ask me anything, Harlan. Always. And to answer your question, I don't remember the exact number of years, but I do know it was a century or so before Damien was made the king."

That...I hadn't expected. "So you're older than Damien?"

Nox narrowed his eyes at me, tugging my hair, though not painfully so. "I'm still young, thank you very much. Damien was the chief of Anubis squad for a while before he became king. I...I pretty much became the Keeper a few weeks after coming to Otherworld. It was a new spot and no one wanted the job, so I volunteered."

Huh. So the position of the king wasn't hereditary. That was interesting. What wasn't surprising was that my mate had volunteered for a potentially dangerous job just because no one else wanted to do it. "Yeah, that sounds like you."

"Oh? So you think you know me that well already?" he asked, brow raised in challenge.

"I know enough to know that I want to spend the rest of my lives with you," I admitted, and a blush stole across his cheeks. He jerked my head back, narrowing his eyes.

"Again with the sappy shit. How do I get you to stop?"

"You could try kissing me," I suggested, and he rolled his eyes.

"That would be positive reinforcement, not a deterrent."

"You can't train me like a dog, Nox."

"But can't I?" he teased, and then he was leaning down and giving me the most awkward, most wonderful kiss of my life.

SIXTEEN

Nox

"Do you sense them?" I asked after a few moments of silence. Even though we didn't need to catch our breaths, I'd needed a few moments to absorb that phenomenal kiss, and as if knowing that, Harlan had given me the time to do it.

"Sense who?" Harlan asked, sitting upright, instantly alert.

"Shhh...not a danger. Just...I think there's a forest spirit living in this park," I said, my voice turning into a whisper even though I was sure the spirit couldn't hear us. Mostly.

"A forest spirit? Really? I've never seen one in person. I didn't even know they still existed." Harlan had a look of utter fascination on his face, looking around as if he expected the spirit to jump out of a tree and shout boo! He was endearing.

"Neither did I. I can't remember the last time one passed through Otherworld." None had in the time I was Keeper; that was for sure.

"Raiden is around 2000 years old. Do you think the spirit is that old? Older?"

"It's totally possible. They were more present in the times when people used to worship nature. Honestly, I wish people still did that. I mean, I don't begrudge them their various Gods, but it's like everyone's forgotten the nature they keep hurting with their development and progress is the same nature that has been nurturing them since humans first existed." I snapped my mouth shut, blushing at my rant. I hadn't intended to do that, but it'd just slipped out.

"I love how passionate you are about this, and I completely agree with you," Harlan said, making my embarrassment disappear in an instant. He wasn't lying, was he? He really did get me. "Do you remember your first life? I heard you forget things the longer you stay in Otherworld."

He acted like it was a casual question, but it was anything but. I could see the tension around his eyes, the way he held himself still waiting for my answer. He wanted to know if he'd one day forget his family. I wished I could assure him he wouldn't, but it wasn't something I could change, no matter how much I wished I could, and I wouldn't lie to him.

"I know I was human, but beyond that? No, I don't remember. But you have to understand I've been in Otherworld for three, maybe four centuries now. The human realm I lived in has changed drastically. My family was gone within a century of my death. I had nothing to hold on to, so I forgot. But you were a supe. Your family is made up of supes, and you can come see them anytime you want. It won't be the same for you." I hadn't noticed how tightly I was squeezing his hands as I spoke—or when I'd grabbed them in the first place—and I loosened my hold now, giving them a much lighter apologetic squeeze.

"That makes sense. And even if, someday, I forgot about them, I think I'd be okay, as long as I have you," he said, his blue eyes looking all the way into my deepest desires and fears.

I groaned to keep up appearances because I couldn't let him know just how much I loved the sappy shit he said, and he simply chuckled, as if he already knew.

I blinked as a drop of water landed on my nose and looked up just as the skies opened up. Oh! Rain! When was the last time I'd been in the rain?

I rushed to my feet, tugging Harlan after me as I stepped into the middle of the clearing where the tree wouldn't keep the rain from drenching us. Turning to Harlan, I grinned up at him. "Let's dance!"

"What?" he asked with a laugh, but I simply stepped away from him and raised my arms up in the air, rocking my hips to the music of the rain, my hair clinging to my face, my clothes drenching almost instantly.

"Come on, Harlan! Dance with me!" I grabbed his hand again, tugging it up with mine. I shrieked when he used the hold to pull me to him, smacking right into his hard muscular chest.

He wrapped an arm around my waist before leading me into the kind of romantic dance I'd only ever seen in movies. He whirled me away from him, twirling me perfectly until I was almost dizzy. Had he learned to dance somewhere? He was awfully good at this, something I hadn't expected.

I was laughing as he pulled me back into his arms, and I looked up into his bright blue eyes, getting caught in the joy and adoration I could see reflected there. This was everything I'd dreamed of. He was everything I'd ever dreamed of.

"Fuck, Harlan. How did I get so lucky?"

"We both got lucky, Trouble. Very, very lucky."

"Trouble, huh?" I asked, liking the nickname more than I probably should.

"Yep. My trouble. My mate. My Nox," he said, each *my* accompanied with a kiss, on each of my cheeks, and one on my nose.

"I can live with that," I murmured, leaning up on my toes to seal it with a kiss. This kiss was different from the one we'd shared under the tree. That one had been full of sweetness and exploration, while this one...this one was pure, unadulterated hunger.

Harlan kissed me like he wanted to consume me, like he wanted to reach every part of me through the kiss. And honestly, it felt like he did. Like he could see all of me laid bare for him.

I pressed closer to him, hitching my leg onto his hip so there was absolutely no space between us. Like he'd done before, he wrapped my other leg around his waist, his palms on my ass as he held me to him, walking forward until he had my back pressed against a tree trunk, all the while kissing me like his life depended on it. Or *not-life*. Whatever. I didn't have the ability to brain right now.

Harlan

"Home," I murmured against his lips. "We need to go home."

Nox's lips curved into a smile, and magic stirred around us. The rain was replaced with warmth and the scent of honey in the air. It was fascinating how quickly it'd become the scent of home.

We were in the cabin, and I didn't waste a moment getting Nox out of his shirt, pulling my own off a moment later. I didn't want to let him go even for a moment, but I also desperately wanted to get him out of his pants. It was a tough decision, but in the end, the need to see him naked won out, and I untangled his legs from my waist before placing him on his feet.

"Pants off, now," I ordered, and he raised a brow at me, cocking his hip and going into what I would dub his brat mode.

"You don't get to order me around just because I'm going to let you fuck me, mister," he sassed, his lower lip sticking out just a little.

I smirked at him, jerking him to me so our naked chests were pressed together. Leaning down, I whispered in his ear, "Even when you're fucking me, I'll still order you around. So you should just get used to it, Trouble."

He sucked in a sharp breath, his eyes jumping to mine. "You would let me top? Even though you've never..."

"Been with a man before? I might not have bottomed before, but I do know my way around toys. Having a gay best friend means you hear a lot about the magic of prostates, and sometimes you get curious. And sometimes, you fall in love with it," I added with a wink, and Nox grinned, his eyes bright with what I assumed were ideas for how he'd use this new knowledge to make my life more interesting.

"I might take you up on that sometime soon. But for now, I want this," he murmured, cupping my erection that was trying to burst out of my jeans, "inside me."

"Can't do that unless you have your pants off, Trouble," I reminded him, and he huffed, stepping back to undress. I did the same, pushing our wet clothes aside with my foot before dragging Nox to the bed.

"On your back," I directed, and he narrowed his eyes at me. I raised my brow in challenge, willing to play along for as long as he wanted. The way his cock was leaking precum, I didn't think he had much patience in him.

He proved me right when he huffed and climbed onto the bed, spreading out like a starfish. I chuckled at the dramatics before climbing between his legs. I grabbed his thighs and tugged him closer, widening his legs as I did. He gasped softly, and I met his gaze as I leaned forward and swallowed his cock, tasting his salty precum.

"I swear to god if you don't get your dick in me soon..." he threatened, trailing off when I placed a finger at the edge of his hole, circling it once. Remembering the very helpful fact that I could use magic still, I used a spell to add some lube to my fingers.

Nox startled when I pressed a finger inside him, grinning when he realized what I'd done. "Magic lube, hell yes! Now get me ready and fuck me already, my knight."

I let his cock slip out of my mouth as I sat up, cocking my head at him. "I thought I was the one giving orders."

"I don't care! Just fuck me before I burst. I've waited too long already," he grumbled, and I wondered if he was referring to this wait or the centuries he'd waited for me, for his mate.

Taking pity on him, I focused on getting him ready, using my fingers and more *magic lube* to prep him. I was curious about something Firey had once mentioned, but I wasn't sure I was ready for that. But one day soon, I wanted to rim Nox until he came.

"I'm ready, I'm ready. Please, Harlan. Fuck me," Nox begged, and I took a moment to look him over, spread out and desperate for my dick.

His hair was a mess, his lips swollen and red, spots of color on his pale cheeks. His fingers were curled tight in the bedsheet, the knuckles white. His spread legs shook slightly as I fucked him with my fingers, his cock standing upright, red and leaking at the tip. He was ready all right.

I pulled my fingers out, replacing them with the tip of my cock. The thought of condoms crossed my mind before I remembered we were both dead and didn't need them.

I pushed into him in one slow thrust, bottoming out so our thighs were pressed together. Fuck, he was so tight.

"Fuuuuck, Harlan. You feel so good. Move, move, move," Nox chanted, and I gave him what he wanted, what we both wanted.

Resting my elbows on either side of him, I hovered over him, thrusting into him at a fast clip. I pressed kisses across his throat, licking at the skin before biting softly. I wanted to leave my mark on him so everyone would know he was mine. I didn't think mate marks were a thing here, or at least I hadn't seen any on the others, something I was curious about. But I could always cover Nox with hickeys and give him new ones when they faded. It wouldn't be a hardship.

"Harder," Nox gasped, and I pulled back, taking in the wild look on his face. He looked completely undone, and I loved it.

"Turn around, on your hands and knees," I ordered, and it was a testament to how badly he needed to come that he followed it without protest.

I grabbed his ass once he was ready, biting his cheek softly before spreading them apart and sliding back into him in one hard thrust. He groaned loudly, and I didn't wait for him to adjust, trusting him to tell me if he needed me to stop.

My fingers dug into his ass as I started thrusting into him at a punishing pace, his whole body shaking as he tried to hold himself up. He failed a minute later, dropping forward so his chest was pressed against the mattress.

Knowing he was close, I grabbed his cock, jacking it at the same pace as I felt my own climax closing in.

"Fuck, fuck, I'm gonna—" Nox moaned as his cock spurted in my hand, his orgasm making his hole squeeze impossibly tight around my dick. It was enough to set me off, and I came deep into his ass as he shuddered through the aftershocks, his body slumped over and loose.

When I felt like I could move without falling apart, I pulled out, watching as my cum leaked out of his ass.

"I'll get a cloth," I murmured softly, but before I could move, Nox stopped me.

"No, wait. Leave it. I...I like feeling your cum. Makes me feel...claimed." His cheeks turned bright red as he spoke, but he'd still said it, and it was the hottest thing I'd ever heard.

I lay down beside him and pulled him into a kiss, keeping it soft and light but doing my best to show him how much I liked that idea.

"We should grab some sleep," I said when we pulled apart. "Lord knows what mess tomorrow will bring. Better be rested."

"After that dicking down? I'm going to sleep like the dead. Which I technically am, so whatever."

I chuckled as he yawned and pulled him into a cuddle. He was asleep a few minutes later, and I followed him soon after, sated and content like never before.

SEVENTEEN

Nox

"Do you think they'll find them soon?" Harlan asked as we made our way to the Brume Villa, and I hummed thoughtfully.

"They know the starting location of at least the guy Connor told them about, so it's possible they found him. We'll find out soon enough."

The moment we entered the lounge, it was clear Lionel and Mazia had found the man they'd gone looking for. It was also clear it hadn't gone well.

"What happened? And how the fuck did you get hurt?" It was common knowledge that we couldn't get hurt in the human realm, unless...

"Fuck. Black magic," I mumbled, answering my own question.

"Yep," Lionel agreed, popping the P. He winced as Reece used his magic to mend his arm, which was clearly broken.

"The guy we went looking for was a troll hybrid. Half-human, half-troll. And unlike Dell, he hadn't been able to fight the dark magic infecting him, so he wasn't thinking straight,"

Mazia, who sat on Lionel's other side, hand on his knee in comfort, explained, her lips pressed in a thin line.

"It wasn't his fault, but it's going to make it harder to help him," Lionel said with a deep sigh, gritting his teeth at whatever pain Reece's healing was causing him.

"So, dark magic can harm you in the human realm?" Harlan asked, and I turned to him, surprised I'd forgotten he was there for a moment.

"Oh yeah. It's the only thing that can hurt us in the human realm."

"Let me get this straight. The only thing that can hurt you is also the one thing you need to fight?" he clarified, and I grinned.

"Good motivation, right?"

He shook his head before turning to the others. "We might have to heal him forcefully if he's not willing, especially if he's close to human establishments."

"We might have to do that. We also don't know how in control the others will be, so we need backup plans. We need people to be searching in bigger groups so they're safer," Reece said, and I nodded. We also needed to get Dell all healed up so we'd have one less thing on our plate.

"Nox, why don't you, Lionel, and Kym go take care of Dell?" Reece suggested, sounding every bit like the King-Consort he was. I'd loved watching him and Artemus grow into their powers.

"But...Harlan?" I asked, glancing up at my mate.

"I need his help to build a ward around the Chasm. With the way things are going, I don't want to leave us unprotected."

I sighed, knowing he was right. Turning to Harlan, I looked up at him. "I'll see you later?"

"Soon. Go help Dell. Make sure he's free of the infection. And afterward, tell him about Mistvale. Let him know he'd always be welcome there."

"I will. Be safe, yeah?"

"I'll be right here when you get back. Look, Lionel's all healed up too. You should get going," Harlan said with a raised brow, and I sighed.

"Yeah, yeah. I'm going," I mumbled as Lionel slowly got to his feet. He joined me just as Kym walked into the room. Someone had probably texted him.

I waved at Harlan before turning to Lionel. "Let's go."

The scene we walked into was not the one I'd been expecting. The cabin door hung open, and there was no sign of Dell or the two squad members who were supposed to be guarding him.

"Who was on duty? Do either of you know?"

Kym pulled out his phone and scrolled through his contacts. "It was Bernard and Felicia. I'm calling Bernie."

The phone rang for just a second before the call was picked up, and Kym asked, "Bernie! Are you okay? Where are you?" He was silent for a moment, listening to Bernie's answer. "Fuck, okay. I'm calling backup. Stay there. We'll be around soon."

"What is it?" I asked as soon as the call ended.

"Dell lost control. There were some hikers nearby, and he was already on edge. Bernie and Fel managed to keep him from attacking anyone, but he's now hiding somewhere in the woods, and they don't know if he's still in his monster form or back in control."

"Fuck. Get Zane. Too many people will freak Dell out. Zane knows how to incapacitate someone without truly hurting them," I suggested, and Kym nodded quickly, dialing Zane.

"Should I fly out and see how they're doing? Provide back-up?" Lionel asked, his wings flexing impatiently.

"Do you feel healed enough to do that?" I asked, eyeing his arm.

"Yep. Reece is an amazing healer."

"If you're sure you'll be okay, go ahead. We'll be there as soon as Zane arrives."

Zane appeared a moment after Lionel had left, their eyes roaming around the place, taking everything in, ready to tackle any danger that might jump out of the shadows.

"They're not here. Come on, Lionel went ahead."

Kym led the way, and we followed him deeper into the woods. Lionel flew over to us, leaping to a tree branch to speak. "He's a little bit on the right, still in his monster form. Kym, any way you can throw fireballs instead? Of your purifying fire, I mean."

Kym frowned, creases forming between his brows. "Not really. I can make fireballs, but I can't aim at all. I end up dropping them every time in practice, or go way off course."

Lionel frowned, but I stared speculatively at Kym, gears turning in my head. "What if you just had to drop the fireballs? You could do it then, right?"

"How will that help?"

"It will when Lionel is holding you mid-air, exactly above Dell," I said with a grin, one that Lionel returned, though Kym didn't look quite sure.

"Oh, that's a great idea. Come on, Kym. It'll be fun."

"I want to see this," Zane piped in, a smirk firmly in place. They clearly didn't expect it to work, and I would prove them wrong.

"Come on. Let's see what we're actually up against before trying anything," I said, and Lionel took to the air again, leading the way.

The Dell I spotted when we reached the tree he'd climbed wasn't the sweet guy I'd talked to before. This creature was...scary. I'd never seen a wendigo in this form before, since when they died, their soul reverted back to their original, human form.

But this form...it was a mix of what zombies looked like on TV—real zombies were just necromancer magic gone wrong—and demons. His skin was gray, with black circles under his eyes, which were a weird, washed-out white, long black claws on his fingers—perfect for ripping through human skin—and bone white antler-like horns sticking out of his head.

He growled when he spotted us, and I caught sight of a mouthful of sharp, pointed teeth. I shuddered at the picture he made, a true monster, and found it hard to comprehend this was the same man who'd looked so scared and unsure the other day.

This was why he was so scared of losing control. Who would ever want that when it made them look and act like this?

"Hey, Dell. It's me, Nox. Remember me?" I tried, hoping there was some part of him that was still in there.

He eyed me with his strange white eyes, but didn't say anything.

"Lionel, Kym, get to work. I'll handle it if he tries to escape," Zane ordered. I hadn't even noticed Lionel had landed behind us, but now he grabbed Kym by the waist and leapt into the sky.

Kym looked ready to hurl, but being a soul collector kept him from actually doing it. They arched over the woods before Lionel steadied himself, hovering over Dell.

I kept talking in an attempt to keep Dell's attention on me. "Hey, Dell. Come on. Don't tell me you forgot this pretty face," I teased, but there was no reaction.

Before I could say anything, the first fireball dropped on him. Instead of rolling off, the ball got absorbed into his skin, as if it could sense the black magic inside him. Kym sent a flurry of fireballs after the experimental one, too quick to allow Dell time to escape.

The wendigo screeched loudly, bits of black ash falling off his skin, as if Kym's magic was literally pulling the dark magic out of him and turning it to ash.

Zane threw a knife before I'd even noticed Dell's attempt to jump out of the tree, and it lodged itself into his clothes, pinning them to the tree. Zane had made sure not to hurt him, and I smiled at them for that. Wren had surely changed them, and for the better.

Kym dropped another few fireballs at him, stopping only when one of them rolled off him, not affecting him now that the black magic had all burned off.

He was still in his wendigo form, though, so I stepped forward, and tried again. "Hey, Dell. Remember me? It's Nox. Can you come back to us, please?"

The wendigo blinked at us for a few moments, before his skin started changing color. His horns slowly sank back into his scalp, his nails turning back to normal. His eyes were the last ones to change, but a moment later, he was staring at me with his deep brown eyes, which immediately widened in horror.

"Oh my god. Please tell me I didn't hurt someone!"

"You didn't!" I rushed to assure him, running forward when he tumbled off the tree, no longer able to hold himself as steadily now that his feet—which I hadn't noticed, but must've also turned to claws—had returned back to their human form.

I helped him to his feet, dusting off the dry leaves that clung to his clothes. "Are you okay? Do you feel better?"

"I'm in control, I promise," he assured me, and I smiled.

"I know. We got rid of all the black magic, so you're safe now."

He blew out a deep breath before eyeing us and Lionel and Kym, who'd just dropped back to the ground, Kym looking a little worse for wear. "What are you people? Even in my...other form, I didn't want to eat you."

I grinned, throwing an arm over his shoulder. "That's a secret. But now that you're okay, how about we get you back to your cabin. There's something I want to tell you before we part ways."

He eyed me warily, but started walking, and we headed back to his cabin. I glanced around, then turned to Zane. "Where are Bernie and Fel?"

"At the cabin. I told them to go ahead and make sure the area was clear," Zane explained. Clear? Of what?

Their raised brows and eyes snapping to Dell and back to me made me go ooooh with realization. Humans, right. Hungry wendigo and all.

"You hungry? Want us to get you some food?" I asked Dell, and he stumbled forward, eyes wide.

"N-no, I'm good. I promise. I won't attack anyone," he tried to assure me, his voice trembling.

"That's not why I asked, kiddo. You need your nutrition, no matter what form you get it in. You said you have a supplier, right? Call them while we're here so I know you'll eat something."

He looked up at me, eyes conflicted and brows furrowed. "Why do you care anyway? I'm a monster."

I rolled my eyes. "Kid, I've seen monsters. I've punished them for their deeds, and I've done it for centuries. Trust me, I know what a true monster looks like, and you aren't one."

Dell's eyes watered, and he looked away, swallowing hard. I gave him a minute to gather himself before we reached his cabin. Then, I pointed toward it. "Go ahead. Get your phone and call your supplier."

He obeyed instantly, and I followed him into the cabin to make sure he actually did it. His voice was soft as he asked the person on the other end to deliver his usual order. A human flesh food delivery service, huh? The world really was turning modern in every aspect. I felt like I'd finally seen everything.

When he was done, I gestured for him to take a seat on the bed. The others had decided to stay outside, so it was just the two of us. Taking the chair, I took his hand in mine.

"You're all healed up now, but I want you to take care of yourself, okay? No starving yourself, or I'll come back here and kick your ass."

The smallest of smiles peeked at his lips, and he dipped his head in agreement.

Smiling in satisfaction, I squeezed his hand. "Now, there's a clan in this town called Mistvale. It's watched over by a dragon, and it's really accepting. If you don't have anything tying you here, you should go check it out. They've extended an invitation to all the supes who got infected."

Dell's eyes went wider the more I spoke, and he finally jerked his hand out of mine, twisting it with his other one in his lap. "I'm not—not fit for that kind of life. I belong here. Alone," his voice was barely audible when he said the last word, but I still heard it, and my heart ached for him.

"No one deserves to be alone, kiddo. I can't force you, but please think about it, okay?"

He nodded, but I had a feeling he wouldn't be going to Mistvale. I guess I'd just have to look out for him myself. Maybe I needed to put in a good word for him with Fate. If anything would pull him away from this life of loneliness, it'd be finding his mate.

"All right then, I better get going. Here, add my number to your phone. I might not always answer instantly, but I'll always get back to you, so text or call me if you need me, okay?"

"I will," he murmured, and I watched as he added my number to his contacts. Satisfied he had a way to contact me, I pulled him to his feet and into a hug. He stiffened instantly, showing how unused he was to simple affection like this, and I made a mental note to beg Fate if I had to. This man needed someone, stat. And I'd play matchmaker for him if I had to.

But before I could do that, I needed to get back to Otherworld, back to my mate.

EIGHTEEN

Harlan

I explained the spell to Reece, showing him how we could use our combined magic to not only build a ward around the tower that stood over the Burning Chasm, but also build it in a way that any dark souls who tried to escape would get stuck to the inner walls of the ward, making it easier for us to send them back.

"That's fascinating. I've had this magic for a while now, and I still don't know everything I can do with it," Reece mused, and I smiled.

"I'd be happy to teach you the spells I know. I'm already teaching Wren some," I offered, and Reece's face lit up, his brown eyes flashing to mine.

"I'd love that. Let's do it once we have a little breathing room."

I nodded, knowing we had no time for magic classes right now.

We spent the next few hours building the ward, but it was slow going. Knowing the dark souls had dug beneath the

Chasm, we couldn't just make a usual dome ward. Instead, we had to build a sphere, one that went deeper than the area they'd already dug up.

Nox had estimated that their digging ended fifty feet below the surface, but we went with seventy just to be safe—and to avoid detection for as long as possible.

When we'd worked for five hours straight, we took a break. While I wasn't hungry or physically tired like Reece, my magic did need some room to breathe. One downside of having your own magic was the very real possibility of burnout, and I wanted to avoid that if I could.

A while ago, Artemus had dropped off some food for his mate, so Reece dug into it while I spread on the grass, staring at the blue sky above.

My eyes slid back to Reece after a while, and I thought about what Nox had told me about Damien and his mates. Their story fascinated me. How Reece had made a deal with Damien to save his husband's—Artemus's—life, not knowing Damien was his mate.

It was just...fascinating. As was the mate mark on Reece's chest. Three snakes followed each other and formed a loopy triangle right over his heart. I was really curious about that mark.

"Can I ask a slightly personal question?" I asked, and Reece looked up at me, his auburn hair ruffling in the breeze.

"Go ahead," he said, waving his water bottle at me in a go on motion.

"Why do you have a mate mark? Maximus or Zane don't; neither do their mates. Unless they all got theirs on their legs, in which case ignore me," I added, and Reece chuckled.

"No, you're right. The others don't have mate marks. I believe it's because mate marks are mostly a physical marker of a bond. A bond can exist without a mate mark, but the mark strengthens it." Reece packed up the food containers as he talked, stopping every few seconds to gesture with his hands.

"Artemus and I are human, and I think like our ability to consume food, Damien also got our ability to be able to be joined by mate bonds. Soul collectors don't have a physical form. They're...spirits, souls. The magic of the realms gives you this form," he said, waving at my body. "But in actuality, you look the way you did when you entered the Chasm. So when your body isn't real, there's no real point of marking it, is there? Since everyone here can see someone's soul, anyone who looks at you two together would know you're mates, which is exactly what a mate mark would do."

I took a few minutes to digest that. It didn't sound possible, that this body I had was made up of magic, and basically an illusion.

"So, you're saying the magic of the realms gave me the ability to come?" I asked with a raised brow, and Reece sputtered, his cheeks pinkening.

"Erm, yes, technically."

"Wow," I murmured, truly shocked. I hadn't expected that. But then again, I was dead. Just because I could do some of the things I did when I was alive didn't mean I was alive.

"Do you think you're ready to get back to it?" Reece asked, cracking his knuckles as he eyed the tower.

"I am, but I think we should get some help. It'll make things easier and faster."

"Wren?" Reece asked with a raised brow, and I nodded. I hadn't had a chance to train him yet, but I was sure that once he knew the spell, he'd be able to use it without a problem.

"I'll text him," I said, and did just that. His reply was almost instant.

Be there in a minute.

Wren showed up just as we reached the tower—we'd walked a bit further away to take our break just in case—and he did not look happy. His blue eyes were full of worry, and I walked closer to him, reining in my urge to comfort him with touch. I didn't know how okay he was with it, and I didn't want to hurt him.

"What's wrong?"

As if he'd expected the question, he showed me a pre-typed text on his phone.

Zane was called in for backup by Nox. I'm worried.

"Fuck," I swore softly, worry for Nox rushing through me. Were they okay? Should I go to them? But Nox would've called me if he needed me, right?

"What's wrong?" Reece asked, realizing something was up.

"They called Zane for backup in the human realm. We're worried about them," I explained, and Reece frowned.

"They'll be okay, don't worry. There's five of them there now. And if they need help, they'll contact us. I know it isn't easy to sit back and do nothing, but we have to let them do their job. What we can do to help is make sure they return to a safer home. What do you say?"

I was all for that, and by the determined look on his face, I'd say so was Wren.

I took the next five minutes to explain the spell to Wren. He caught up faster than Reece had, his warlock training kicking in, and before long, the three of us were working on the ward again, building a wall of magic that would protect our men and everyone in Otherworld—and possibly the human realm—from the evil beneath us.

I heard murmurs when we'd been working for an hour or so, but I ignored it, focusing on the ward. The others seem to do the same, but with Wren's help and not having to fight the dark magic that had leaked underground, we finished the ward much faster.

It must've taken us half the time to get it set up, and then it was just a matter of adding a small spell that made it so only Reece, Artemus, Damien, and Lionel would be able to go in or out. I didn't know what Nox would say about not being allowed near his workplace, but Reece had insisted it was the only way to make sure Nox didn't try to return.

I stretched my arms above my head, feeling magically exhausted. I wanted to head to our cabin and sleep for at least ten hours, but before that I needed to make sure Nox was okay.

I'd taken all of two steps toward the Brume Villa when he appeared a few steps away, closing the distance between us with a grin on his face. "I see you're done. I came up before, but you looked so sexy all focused on your work, so I just sat on the grass and drooled for a bit."

I chuckled at his statement, pulling him into a hug. "I heard you needed backup. Are you okay? Did anyone get hurt?"

"We're all fine, don't worry. Dell lost control, but I think he was mostly scared. We needed Zane because they can neutralize someone without hurting them, and we needed that to heal Dell."

"That makes sense. Is Dell okay now? Free of dark magic?"

"Yep, completely. I told him about Mistvale, but I don't think he'll listen. I'm gonna keep watch over him, though. He needs someone who cares about him. I'm also gonna put in a good word for him when Fate next drops by."

I'd heard about Fate and their brother, the King of Afterworld, but I didn't realize they were that close.

"You can do that? It's not against the rules or something?"

Nox made a face, shrugging as he snuck his arm through my elbow, tugging me toward our cabin. I fell in step with him, pulling him tighter against me. "It's not, not really. I'm not going to ask them to change his future or anything, just bring him into their line of sight so they can maybe help him a little. They did that with the Mistvale bunch too. When Fate likes someone, they try to make their lives happier like that."

That did explain how so many people ended up finding their mates when they came to Mistvale. In a way, so had I, just in a completely different situation.

"Well, I hope Fate helps him, then. He looked like he could use it. On another note, how can you feel like your whole body hurts when you technically don't have a body?" I demanded, and Nox laughed, leaning into me.

"Magical exhaustion, huh? I assumed you'd be tired after that, so I set something up for you in our cabin. Come on, just a few more steps."

"We could've magicked there," I grumbled, only now realizing this. It would've used my soul collector magic, so it's not like it would've strained my already tired magic muscles.

"But then we would've missed this nice romantic walk we had," Nox said with a pout, and I couldn't help but smile at him. Lord, he was adorable.

Walking into the cabin, I breathed in the scent of lavender, turning to eye Nox curiously. What had he done?

"Come on, come on." He tugged me further in, stopping in the bathroom and splaying out his hands toward the setup. "Ta-da!"

There were candles everywhere, lighting up the room in a warm, yellow glow. The bathtub was full, with what looked like bath bombs and oil waiting in a basket on the rim.

"A bath?" I asked curiously, my hands already unbuckling my belt.

"I thought we could have one together. I got the bath bombs from Arty. There's a glitter one, a bubbles one, and a simple one. The oils are supposed to be energizing, though I don't think they'll work for us. They still smell good, though."

I grinned at his chatter, then raised a brow. "Shouldn't you be getting naked so you can join me?"

He was immediately pushing his pants off, and I took the moment to study the bath bombs. Knowing Nox, I dropped both the glitter and bubble ones into the water, watching as they burst into an explosion of color and bubbles.

"Awesome!" Nox said with a grin when he saw what I'd done, and I shook my head as he added the oils.

"You first, so I can use you like a pillow," Nox said, and I complied, stepping into the tub and sinking into the warm water.

"Hmm, this feels good," I murmured, closing my eyes to enjoy the warmth.

The water splashed around a little as Nox joined me, his body fitting perfectly against mine. I wrapped my arms around him, pulling him in so he lay on my chest. Pressing a kiss to the top of his shoulder, I said, "Thank you for doing this, Trouble."

"I didn't do it for you," Nox said with a scoff. "I did it for the naked cuddles."

"Of course," I agreed with a smirk. "Can we add naked making out to that list?"

"Fuck yes!" Nox turned over, somehow managing to do it without dislodging too much of the water. Gripping the tub edge on either side of my head, he leaned forward...and immediately slipped in the soapy water, slamming face first into my shoulder.

"Oof," he gasped, jerking up straight and rubbing his nose with his palm and smearing it with the foam his hands were covered in.

Laughing, I took some more of the soapy bubbles and gave him a beard to go with the mustache. "There. Now you look like Santa Claus."

His eyes narrowed at me, his hands falling away from his face. "Oh, so that's how you want to play it, huh? Okay, I'll play."

Before I could react, he was rubbing handfuls of foam onto my face, and I was laughing too hard to fight him. I pushed him away, but he was determined to cover me in bubbles.

Grabbing him around the waist, I flipped us so he was under me, holding him steady as I covered the parts of his face that weren't underwater with bubbles. He was laughing too hard to fight anyway, and knowing he couldn't drown made it easy to hold him in the water as I ended up tickling him until he was gasping with laughter.

"Stop, stop, stop! I give!" he exclaimed, and I pulled him up, wiping the soap from his face. His cheeks were flushed, eyes bright, and the moment he was bubble-free, he attacked me with an enthusiastic kiss, crawling into my lap. I was grateful for his extra-large tub as he settled comfortably, throwing his arms around my neck as he deepened the kiss.

I let him take the lead, just enjoying being kissed by my mate. I didn't always need to be in control.

After a while, we washed up and crawled into bed, snuggling close. We were both exhausted for different reasons, so after we'd shared another kiss, I pulled Nox closer, spooning around him as he sighed happily, and closed my eyes. Sleep didn't take long to come, and with Nox secure in my arms, I slept like the dead.

NINETEEN

Nox

"So, let me get this straight. You and Reece just decided, without even asking my opinion, that I shouldn't be allowed near the Chasm? I mean, I agree I made a mistake, but I have still been the Keeper of the Chasm for longer than you've been alive. You had no right to do that," I fumed, feeling more betrayed than angry, to be honest. Unlike what I'd expected, I wasn't eager to get back to work. But not wanting to go back was still my choice, or it had been until these two took it away from me.

Harlan stepped closer, though he didn't try to touch me, probably sensing I wouldn't let him. "I'm sorry. It wasn't really my choice, I promise. Reece decided it'd be best for you, and I didn't know if it was my place to argue. But tell me one thing, Nox, and be honest."

I narrowed my eyes at him. "I'd never lie to you."

He smiled at that, and I had to work hard to hold on to my annoyance. His smile was just a little too sexy, the bastard. "I know. Tell me, Nox, did you really enjoy your job? Did you like it?"

I opened my mouth, ready to answer, but then my shoulders slumped as I realized my answer wasn't true anymore. At one point, I had enjoyed it. I'd felt fulfilled, like I was doing something important. But now? Now it just felt like a chore, and being so close to all that darkness messed with me in ways that I was only now realizing, after being away from the Chasm for more than a week.

"I did, once. But I don't anymore. It's lonely. And being that close to the Chasm messes up my emotions."

This time, Harlan did close the distance between us, and I let him, sinking into the hug he offered. My arms wrapped around his waist as his palm rubbed my back, and he pressed a kiss to the top of my head.

"What if you didn't have to be the Keeper anymore? What if there was no need for a Keeper at all?" Harlan asked after a moment, and I pulled back to look at him, puzzled.

"What do you mean?"

"The ward Reece, Wren, and I built is pretty strong, if I do say so myself. What if, after this is all over, we could code it so any dark soul would only be able to get inside, not leave, and a pure soul could travel in and out without a problem? With some changes to the ward you and Artemus put on the tower, we could make it so any soul collector would be able to dump the souls into the Chasm."

I thought about that, a world where I wouldn't have to be the Keeper. It didn't sound bad.

"What would I do if I wasn't the Keeper?" I asked, frowning. It was all I'd ever known in this realm.

"You could join me on Max's squad. We could roam all over the human realm together, fighting the real monsters," Harlan offered, and my eyes lit up.

"We could be superheroes!" I gasped, and he chuckled, a wry smile on his face.

"Yes, that's exactly what I meant. Think about it, yeah? You don't need to decide just yet. I haven't mentioned my idea to anyone."

I squeezed him and smacked a kiss on his cheek for that, before something trickled through the back of my mind.

"Oh shit! We should get going. Lionel, Kym, and Max are supposed to go heal the troll today. I want to go with them." When I'd returned yesterday, Lionel had informed me they were waiting for Damien's go ahead. Damien had been in Afterworld then, updating King Tharion about everything we'd discovered so far. He should be back by now, and knowing the urgency of the situation, he'd have told them to go.

"Come on, then," Harlan said, taking my hand. Magic stirred around us, and then we were in the lounge of the Brume Villa.

"Did they leave? Lionel and the others?" I demanded of Vaishnavi, who was writing something on her tablet. She looked up when I spoke, and blinked once, shaking her head slightly.

"Oh yeah, they did, a few minutes ago. But get this. Remember how Cynthia said one of the supes is a fae?"

"Yeah?" I asked warily, not trusting the spark in her eyes.

"Well, she lied. Or, even she didn't know the truth."

"What truth?" I demanded when it was clear she was a teasing tease who teased.

"He's not truly fae. Or he's part fae, just enough to have a very strong glamor," she explained, giddiness filling her voice.

"So what is he, then?" Harlan asked, looking as curious as I felt.

"This," Vaishnavi declared, turning her tablet to us, where a picture was prominently displayed on the screen.

"Is that..." Harlan trailed off, his arm tightening around me.

"A kraken?" I finished for him, my mind blanking for a moment before it came back online. "A fucking kraken? Are you kidding me right now? And the bitch witch found him by dumb luck? Is that what you're telling me? What. The. Fuck."

I shook my head, slipping out of Harlan's hold because I needed to walk off this sudden rush of energy. A wendigo, a troll, a motherfucking kraken, a kelpie, a wyvern...

"Monsters," I murmured, and both of them looked up at me.

"What?" Harlan asked, walking closer to me.

"Dell, the troll, the others...they're all monsters. Like, not really of course. You've met Dell. But wendigos are one of the most brutal creatures of the human realm, the trolls are violent as fuck, kelpies are known for luring unsuspecting humans into the water, wyverns are the more violent, wilder cousins of dragons, and we all know how famous krakens are for toppling over whole ships. My point is they picked beings who would easily be able to harm or lure humans. Even fae are known for tricking humans, which explains why they picked him."

"Huh, that does make sense," Vaishnavi mused, looking through her tablet again. "The kraken is in London, by the way. Taking a nice little dip in the Thames."

"Fuck. Who found him?" I asked, and she sighed.

"Caelan and a few of Max's men. They're still there. keeping an eye on the situation. They managed to lure the kraken into deeper waters, away from the humans, but they can't get through to him either. The black magic in their system is making them more volatile."

"Fuck. I wish we had more than just Kym to help these people. He can't be everywhere, and he can't work indefinitely. These people need help," I growled, and Harlan squeezed my shoulder, tipping my head up.

"We'll figure it out, all right? They'll get the help they need."

I nodded, sighing. I rested my forehead against his chest, soaking in his steadiness and hoping it'd leech out some of my jittery nerves.

"Aww, you two are adorable," Vee declared, and I pulled back to glare at her.

"Do not call me that," I ordered her, but she merely stood up and gave me a little wave.

"A-do-rable," she repeated, before magicking away like a coward.

Harlan chuckled before pulling me back into a hug. "Down, tiger. You're a fierce alpha male. How's that?"

"I'm a fierce, sexy alpha male," I corrected him, and he grinned widely.

"That too," he agreed, before pulling me into a kiss. Hmm, I could get used to this. Hell, who was I kidding? I already was.

Harlan

It was evening before Lionel, Kym, and Max returned, looking absolutely exhausted and a little disgruntled.

"Did it go well?" I asked as Nox jumped up, done with sitting still now that they were here. He rushed over to Lionel as Kym and Max slumped on the couch across from me, exhaustion clear on their faces.

"Eh, that's up for debate. He's a half-troll, so nowhere as huge as a true troll would be, but he's a damn good fighter. And very stealthy too."

"I had to convince Mr. Overprotective over here to even let me within firing range of him," Kym mumbled, his head resting on Max's shoulder. He looked like he'd fall asleep at any moment, and the look Max gave me could easily be translated to *does it look like I was wrong?*

I shook my head with a smile, eyeing my own risk-taker as he conversed with Lionel. It was clear we'd need to revisit the troll, but there was another equally, if not more important person we needed to help.

"They found the third one today. The fae guy, who is actually a kraken," I told Maximus, and his eyes widened.

"What the fuck? Seriously?" he demanded, and I told him everything Vaishnavi had told us.

"Fucking hell." He eyed Kym, who'd already fallen asleep, his face lined with worry.

"Wren and I should come with you when you go to heal the kraken. We can lend Kym our magic so he doesn't exhaust himself completely," I offered, knowing Wren wouldn't mind. He might keep to himself, but I knew he cared about his new family.

"This is still better than what happened when he turned a black soul gray, but I'll welcome any help I can get," Max answered, a grateful smile on his face.

"Just let us know when, and we'll be there."

"As much as I'd like to, we can't leave it for too long. The kraken is too close to humans. Hopefully, a good night's sleep will have him recharged. If not, we'll head out tomorrow evening."

"Sounds good to me. I'll talk to Nox later. You should go ahead and get some sleep too," I suggested, and he rubbed a palm over his face, nodding.

"Yeah, you're right. See you tomorrow, Harlan."

I waved him off as he picked Kym up—who stayed sleeping, clearly too exhausted to wake up—and magicked up to their room.

Nox jumped on the couch beside me, his eyes wide. "Do you think they're all like Dell? Sweet guys who were rejected by the people who should've cared about them?"

"In my experience, most bad guys usually have a painful backstory that makes them that way," I mused, and Nox raised a brow at me.

"And is your experience in any way related to superhero movies?"

I laughed, not expecting that. Then again, Nox did have a habit of doing the unexpected. I watched him, the mischievous sparkle in his eyes, the way his lips twitched with a barely restrained smile, and decided that just this once, I wanted to do the unexpected. I wanted to be the one who shocked him.

Tipping his head up, I met his gorgeous gray eyes, and spoke with all the sincerity I possessed. "I love you, Trouble."

His eyes widened, his lips parting slightly, and he went stock still, not a hair moving on his head. Had I truly shocked him that badly? He would've been expecting it on some level, right?

As quickly as he'd turned into a statue, he jumped me, his lips crashing on mine with all the desperation of a drowning man reaching for the surface. I wrapped my arms tighter around him, and he crawled on top of me, his hands falling to either side of me as he hovered over me, his lips brushing against mine as he demanded, voice hoarse, "Do you mean it?"

"I'd never lie to you," I told him, repeating his words from earlier, and a wide grin spread across his lips. He kissed me again, and I could practically taste his joy on his lips, feel it in my heart. Was this what being bonded felt like?

I kissed him with everything I had, and he gave back just as good as he got. Magic stirred around us, and then we were in our cabin, in our bed, with Nox still on top of me.

He pulled back just enough to meet my eyes, his own turning molten silver with desire as they roamed over my face. "I want to be inside you. Will you let me?"

"Anything you want," I promised him. I might've never bottomed before, but I knew enough about myself to know I'd love having Nox inside me, love it when he came inside me and marked me as his. "Fuck me, Nox. Make me yours."

Nox made a soft, growl-like sound in the back of his throat before he was on me again, his lips landing on my jaw as he trailed kisses down to the base of my neck, biting and licking as his hands worked on unbuttoning my jeans.

I arched my neck to give him better access, and he hummed softly, pulling away long enough to get rid of both our pants before he was on me again, tasting every bit of my skin he could find, murmuring words like "sexy" and "so hot" between licks and bites.

He was slowly driving me crazy, and I wasn't quite sure I'd be able to hold on until he was inside me. Fuck, did I love this man.

TWENTY

Nox

I'd known my mate was sex on legs from the moment I first saw him, but nothing beat having him spread out before me like this, waiting for me to devour him. He looked delicious, so worked up and ready, and I wanted to keep teasing him, keep driving him crazy.

I sat back on my heels, surveying my handiwork. The hickeys would heal before long, but I loved seeing my marks on him. He watched me with glazed eyes that narrowed when I continued to do nothing, and he growled. "I swear to god, Nox, if you don't fuck me right now..."

"What? What will you do?" I teased, leaning over him so we were nose to nose. "Will you not kiss me for a week?" I asked, brushing my lips against his. "Or will you keep me away from this gorgeous cock of yours?" I ran my fingers up his hard length, slowly licking the drops of precum that I collected.

"Nox," Harlan almost whined. I hadn't known this big, burly man could make that kind of sound. "Please," he added, and how could I resist that?

"Shhh...I'll give you what you need, I promise. Now, magic me some lube," I ordered, holding my palm out.

He huffed a chuckle and mumbled a spell, filling my hand with lavender-scented lube.

"Nice," I commented, moving down his body until I was staring at his hole. I ran a dry finger around the pucker, and his hole twitched, making me smile. Covering my finger in lube, I slipped it inside, humming at how tight he felt. A rush of pride filled me to the brim at the realization that I'd be the only person to ever touch him like this, to fill him with my cum. Fuck, that was a sexy thought.

Leaning down, I pulled his cock into my mouth as I slid another finger into him, teasing him with light licks, bobbing my head up and down his length with my lips loosely wrapped around him to keep him on the edge.

"If you keep doing that, I'm going to cum before you get inside me," Harlan growled, and I glanced up at him, at his flushed cheeks and his perked-up nipples, at the way his fists were curled into the sheets.

Challenge accepted.

I doubled down on my efforts, tightening my lips around his dick as I added a third finger inside him. I fucked him with my fingers as I blew him, working in tandem to push him over the edge.

His fingers slid into my hair, gripping tightly as he took control, fucking my mouth as I fucked his ass. His hips stuttered, and he gave a shout as his warm, salty cum filled my mouth. I swallowed quickly, not wanting to waste a single drop. I sucked the last drops out of him before pulling away, and he fell back onto the bed, his eyes closed and a sated look on his face.

Then his eyes opened and met mine, the blue impossibly bright. "Fuck me, Nox. Now."

This time, I didn't protest at all. I simply covered my cock with the remaining lube and crawled over Harlan so I could look into his eyes as I slid into him, slowly, oh so slowly.

I could go hard and fast like I liked it, but I wanted to take this slow. I didn't just want to fuck him—I wanted to make love to him. Because he'd said he loved me, and every wisp of my soul loved him too.

Harlan's eyelids fluttered as I bottomed out inside him, and I stayed like that as I pressed a kiss to his lips, one he readily returned. The kiss was deep and full of feelings, full of love. I could taste it in the way he kissed me, the way his palm came up to cup my head carefully, as if I was precious to him.

When I pulled back, I could see all those emotions and more in Harlan's eyes, and I had to tell him how I felt, even if he could read it just as clearly in my eyes. "I love you, Harlan."

"I know," he said with a little smirk, and I smacked him on his ridiculously muscular chest, which just made him laugh. "I love you too, Trouble. Now, move."

"Yeah, yeah," I mumbled, feeling my cheeks heat even as I slowly slid almost all the way out of him before thrusting back into him. I set up a slow, steady pace, driving us both crazy as Harlan's cock woke up and joined the fun again.

I'd been fucked hard many times, and I'd fucked someone a couple of times too, but nothing had felt like this. Making love to Harlan was on a level of its own, and nothing could compare. Except maybe getting fucked into the mattress by him.

As I felt my climax closing in, I wrapped my hand around his cock while leaning down to kiss him. I jerked him off as I slid my tongue inside his mouth, tasting him and letting him taste himself on me.

I rested my forehead on his as my orgasm appeared out of nowhere, murmuring his name as I filled him with my cum.

"Fuck, Nox," he groaned softly, and then he was coming in my hand, his cum coating my hand and his abdomen.

"Fuck, you look sexy when you come," I murmured, kissing him chastely as he trembled with aftershocks.

I only pulled away when my softened cock slipped out of him and sat up, taking in the view of him all sexed up and debauched.

Spotting my phone on the floor—how did it even get there?—I grabbed it, turning on the camera and taking a quick picture while Harlan raised a brow at me.

"Just adding it to my collection of sexy men I got all sexed up," I teased, and his eyes narrowed. With speed he shouldn't have a minute after coming—for the second time in a row at that—he sat up and grabbed the phone from my hand.

I watched, amused, as he swiped through my gallery, only to realize his was the only picture in there. I really didn't use my phone often, but I might have to start carrying it around so I could take sexy pics of my man.

"You are pure trouble," Harlan said as he threw the phone onto the mattress and reached for me. I jumped out of bed with a laugh, walking backward toward the bathroom.

"I'll get a washcloth for you. Just sit there and look pretty," I told him, grinning when he rolled his eyes.

I cleaned up quickly, grabbing a washcloth for Harlan like I'd promised. When I returned, he'd made the bed and lay starfished on it, his eyes on the ceiling. He glanced at me when I reached the bed and smiled softly.

Climbing onto the bed, I wiped him clean, taking extra care around his hole, though magic would've healed any soreness he'd had by now. When I was done, I threw the cloth on the floor to take care of later and curled up beside Harlan.

He instantly turned on his side, wrapping an arm around me and pulling me close so our chests were pressed together.

I enjoyed just being in his space, feeling content in a way I'd never felt before. I was still very much hopped up on the pleasure rush, though, and I didn't think I'd be sleeping for a while. I hoped neither would Harlan.

Harlan

After a few minutes of silence, it was clear Nox had had enough of it. He looked up at me and asked, "Whatcha thinking?"

I smiled at him, loving how predictable yet utterly unpredictable he was. I hadn't realized I needed someone like him in my life, someone who would shake things up and make me see the world differently.

"Well, I was thinking about why we can still feel pain, but now I'm thinking about how glad I'm to have you in my life, or afterlife."

Nox gave a cocky grin, his eyes filling with heat. "We'll come back to that second part, but first, how did I know you were still thinking about that? Why does it bother you so much?"

I frowned, honestly unsure of the answer myself. "I don't know. I think it's mostly the fact that everyone talks about death as if you'd be free of all pain and suffering once you reach it, and I'm finding it a little hard to reconcile that that's not the case."

"Well, that thinking is not exactly wrong. You are free of the suffering and pain you had as a human, in a way. Like, emotional suffering. As for physically getting hurt, that can only happen to us Otherworlders. Once you get to Afterworld, it's all nice and peachy."

"Why do you say that with such distaste?" I asked and then immediately shook my head. "Let me guess. Because nice and peachy is boring?"

"Awww, you do get me!" Nox grinned before making a face. "Nice is boring. I like adventure and danger and doing things. In Afterworld, people just sit around and do nothing all day. I think. I've only been there a few times, and it did not appeal to me. At all."

"We're never going to Afterworld. Got it," I said with a laugh, and he met my eyes, worry replacing some of his earlier distaste.

"But we could, if you want to go," he said, sounding completely sincere, and I smiled, tucking his hair behind his ear before cupping his face.

"You know what I realized?" I asked, and he blinked, his gray eyes looking all the way into my soul, or maybe even deeper if that was possible.

"What?" he asked finally, and I blinked, realizing I'd lost myself in his gaze. Why was that so easy to do? It took me a moment to remember what we were talking about, but then I smiled.

"I realized that I like having a little adventure and trouble in my life."

Nox grinned widely as if I'd given him the greatest gift I could, and I bopped him on the nose because he looked too adorable not to.

"Well, then you're lucky you got me," Nox said, smirking wide.

"Yeah, I'm very lucky indeed."

We were quiet for a few minutes, but Nox kept twitching, telling me he was still awake.

"What are you thinking about?" I asked, and he smiled, probably because I'd thrown his question back at him.

"Just about tomorrow. I keep thinking about all these guys they targeted. How much their lives were affected by this infection. Vaishnavi is doing more research about the kraken, but I think he had a good life in London as a fae. He must've lived alone to be targeted, but he had a life, Harlan. They all did."

The worry on Nox's face had me pulling him even tighter against me, and I pressed a kiss on his forehead before pulling back and saying, "Under all that sass and snark, you hide a really big heart, Nox."

His cheeks flushed at the praise, eyes turning downcast, and I tipped his chin up, smiling at him. "Are you turning shy on me now?"

That lit him right up. His eyes narrowed, and he stuck his tongue out at me. "I'm not shy, thank you very much."

I chuckled, running my palm down his back to settle him. "Sure, of course. And as for those supes, we'll help them, okay? Tomorrow, we'll help Silas, and then we'll help the kraken, and then the other two as soon as they're found. We'll make sure they all get to go back to their lives, okay?"

Nox nodded, sighing deeply before snuggling into me. He stuck his face into the crook of my neck, and I rubbed his back, feeling thankful all over again that this man was mine.

Even when he was reckless, he did it for family, for the people he cared about. He had a big personality, and an even bigger heart, and I was a lucky man to have my very own place in it.

TWENTY-ONE

Nox

"Duck, duck, duck!" I shouted, and Kym rolled to the ground a moment before Silas's huge arm swung at the spot he'd been standing. Silas-the-troll made a low, grunting sound as he pulled back, his flinty black eyes trained on Kym.

Kym readied another fireball as Lionel flew into the troll's line of sight, pulling his attention to himself. As a half-troll, Silas wasn't as big as a true troll, which was a lucky break for us. He stood just shy of eight feet tall in this form, his head covered in shaggy black hair, the rest of his body pale and almost naked. I wasn't really sure if I could call the scrap of cloth covering his privates underwear. I'd have to ask Harlan's opinion later.

"Harlan, stand by to help Kym, okay?" I said to him, my eyes on Silas.

"Why do I get the feeling you're about to do something reckless?" Harlan asked, his voice full of wariness.

"It's because you know me so well, my knight," I answered, shooting him a grin before turning around and running straight at the troll's back.

Soul collectors could do a lot of things in the human realm that they couldn't do anywhere else. I used one of the tricks to boost my jump as I reached Silas, latching onto his back as Lionel held his complete attention.

Silas jerked under me, his head turning in an attempt to see who was behind him.

"Hey, Silas!" I called, putting all the cheer I could into my voice. "My name's Nox. I know it doesn't feel like it, but we're here to help, I promise."

My words seemed to go straight over his head, and I barely evaded his meaty paw as he smacked the back of his neck with it, as if intending to squash me like an annoying fly.

I hung onto his shoulder, my legs dangling in the air. It wouldn't hurt if I fell, but it would hurt if Silas smacked me while I was falling, and I'd rather not give him the chance to do that.

Tightening my grip on his shoulder, I climbed back up onto his back. Lionel's and my distraction tactic seemed to be working because I could see Kym busy throwing fireballs at his legs, Harlan a strong silent support at his back.

"Hurry up! I'm not loving this game very much," I called out to the two, and Harlan looked up at me.

"Ten minutes! Kym needs ten more minutes."

"Gotcha. Do you know any good games trolls like to play?" I asked, and Harlan made that face he always did whenever I said something *crazy*.

"Yeah. They love the one called squishing thy enemies in thy palms," Harlan deadpanned, and I grinned. Aww, I loved this man.

"Hey, Silas. You see that man over there? He's my mate. If you're a good boy and don't hurt anyone, I'll talk to someone who can help you find yours. How's that for a trade?" I asked, but of course, he ignored me. Or rather, he ignored my words and tried to squash me again.

Fifteen minutes later, I was all buzzed up while the rest of the guys looked exhausted beyond belief. Silas sat in the patch of grass he'd trampled, looking nothing like his troll form. He was young, and looked like he still retained some baby fat, his cheeks round and his middle a little chubby. He was a cute kid, and I wanted to kill the dead queen of Underworld for what she'd done to these supes.

I walked over, settling on the grass beside him. "You okay?" I asked, keeping my voice low.

He dipped his head in a nod, his black eyes flashing to meet mine for a split second before he looked away. He had a mask covering the lower half of his face, something he'd put on the moment he'd turned back. I assumed it was to hide the small tusks he had sticking out of his mouth, though I thought they made him look cuter. "I feel much better. More in control. Thank you. I don't even know what happened to me."

I explained in as much detail as I was allowed to give him, holding back everything about the realms. When I was done, it was clear I'd overwhelmed him, and I patted his back, hoping I hadn't scared him too much.

"You're okay now. We've hunted down the people who did this, so you're in no danger, all right? If you need a safe place to go, there's a town called Mistvale that's a haven for supes. Their clan leader offers safety and home to any supe in need."

"I'm not really the kind of person people want in their clans," Silas murmured, eyes trained on the ground in front of him.

"Trust me, they're different. Just think about it, okay?"

Silas nodded again and then looked up at me, his dark eyes worried and so full of innocence. "Are you leaving?"

I took in the way he held himself, his arms tight around his knees as if bracing himself. I shook my head, giving him a smile. "Not right away. I just need to talk to my teammates."

"And your mate?" he asked, eyes flicking to Harlan.

I blinked at him, wondering how he knew, before I remembered telling him. "You heard that?"

His cheeks flushed, and he looked away. "I could hear you, but I wasn't in control of my body. I swear."

"I understand. And yes, he's my mate. I'll be right back, okay?"

Silas nodded, and I stood up, walking over to the three where they stood talking in low voices.

"Ready to leave? We're planning to check on the kraken situation before we go home so Kym is prepared for tomorrow." Harlan said, eyes lighting up at the thought of seeing the kraken. He took my hand in his and pulled me close, and I smiled, leaning up to press a kiss to his lips before pulling away.

"Not yet. I'm staying here with Silas for a bit. You should go ahead," I said, and his brows furrowed.

"I can stay with you," he offered, but I shook my head. He clearly wanted to see the kraken, and I wasn't about to steal the opportunity from him.

"Nah, you go on ahead. Get me on your way back and we'll head home together, okay?"

Harlan sighed before nodding, pulling me into a hug and holding on for a few seconds before letting go. He stared into my eyes for a long moment before saying, "Do not do anything reckless while I'm gone. Got it?"

I gave him a naughty grin and saluted. "Sir, yes sir!"

He merely rolled his eyes before turning to the others, who'd been patiently waiting for us to be done.

Lionel smirked at me, mouthing, *Nox is in loveee.*

I stuck my tongue out at him, and he chuckled.

Kym, who was the most tired of us all, merely leaned against a tree trunk, watching us goof off with a tired smile on his face.

"Go, before Kym falls asleep," I said, and Harlan nodded, pressing a kiss to my forehead.

Then they were gone, and I turned back to Silas, wondering what mischief I could get up to with a half-troll. There were so many fun options.

Harlan

The kraken situation had both good news and bad news for us.

The good news was that the kraken didn't seem interested in coming to the surface or anywhere near the humans, at least for now.

The bad news was he'd need more firepower than what Kym had, even with Wren and me boosting him. Especially because he was underwater, and bringing him out of it might prove even riskier. Maybe I could portal him to a desert location? I'd never made a portal that big, but it was an idea worth trying.

"I can trap him in a ward so he's unable to go to the surface," I suggested, and Lionel looked thoughtful. We'd all magicked underwater since Lionel had known the exact location of the kraken and it'd seemed easier than swimming, and I was glad we didn't need to breathe, even though I instinctively wanted to. I hadn't realized I'd kept up the habit until I consciously needed to hold my breath. Another fascinating aspect of being dead. Also, apparently I didn't need air to talk either, being dead and all. Who would've thought?

Being this deep underwater was fascinating. The water was much darker down here, and I guessed it was magic—again—that allowed us to see so clearly at such depth.

Fishes swam around us, big and small, not giving a shit about the weird creatures just chilling in their water.

"That's a good idea, actually. We'll need time to figure out how else to boost Kym's power, and the last thing we need is humans catching sight of the big, octopus monster," Lionel grumbled, eyeing the kraken warily. He seemed pretty peaceful right now, stationary like he'd been since we arrived. Now that I looked more closely, I could see some fishes...stuck on him? I'd read about fishes who attached themselves to larger ones like sharks and ate their scraps. Was that what this was? And the kraken was *allowing* it?

"That's true. All right, back up. Give me some space to work with. I'll also put a look-away spell in the ward so humans don't see him," I said, and Lionel gave me a thumbs up, his brown hair floating in a halo above him. If Nox was here, I was sure he would've found a dozen ways to tease him about it.

As I watched, Lionel grabbed Kym's arm and tugged him away. Apparently, Kym couldn't swim, and he was finding it hard to steer himself. Guess there were some things magic couldn't help you with.

I eyed the area around the kraken, mapping out the dimensions of the ward in my mind before starting the spell. I weaved it with enough space so the kraken wouldn't be completely packed in and have a little moving space.

When the ward fell into place and my magic settled, the kraken's eyes flicked open, forcing me to take a few steps back as I waited for his reaction to being trapped. My feet sank into the soft riverbed, and I had to jerk my foot out of the mud, forcing myself to stay afloat. It was a good thing I'd learned to swim at an early age, though I'd never known I'd need those skills *after* my death.

One long tentacle extended out of his curled-up body, tapping against the edge of my ward. I waited for him to react, to get violent, but instead he simply...went back to sleep.

I tilted my head, confused. Had we gotten the wrong kraken somehow?

I forced my eyes to look beyond the surface of his body, deeper inside him.

Max had explained the difference between a dark soul and an infected one to me. He'd said that while a dark soul's color was charcoal black, an infected soul's color was more inky or oily. And I could see it clearly on the kraken, the way the trips of inky black clung to his white soul. But unlike Dell and Silas, his soul wasn't covered in it, not as thoroughly. Was he...fighting the infection? Did he know something was wrong with him? Was that why he was being complacent?

"If you can hear and understand me," I called out, hoping I was right, "we aren't here to harm you. We want to heal you, but we need some time. Please be patient, and keep doing whatever you're doing to fight the infection."

"Are you serious? He's really fighting it?" Kym asked, and I turned as Lionel swam closer, tugging Kym along.

"Look at his soul. The dark magic isn't as firmly embedded in him as it was in the others," I explained, and both of them repeated what I'd done, realization crossing their faces.

"This might make things easier," Lionel murmured, and I had to agree.

"But what if we come back tomorrow and he has lost it by then? It happened with Dell," Kym said, and it was a possibility we couldn't ignore. But it was also true that Kym would burn out if he tried to heal the kraken now, and we still had two more supes to find and heal.

"It's a risk we'll have to take, Kym. We'll get here bright and early, okay? Why don't you two get back home and get some sleep? I'll update the guys above keeping watch and then go get Nox."

"Lord knows what trouble he would've found by now," Lionel joked, but I was honestly worried about what I might find.

Once they'd left, I swam up to the surface, though magicking up would've been a lot faster considering how deep I was, and told the guys standing guard about the ward. I didn't begrudge them their job. At all. Using a quick spell to dry myself, I magicked back to Nox, curious what he was up to.

When I arrived back at the clearing we'd left Nox and Silas in, my eyes immediately latched onto Nox, who was, for some unfathomable reason, climbing a tree. He was way too high for my liking, and I wondered just what he was up to.

It was only then that I spotted Silas standing beneath the tree in his troll form, clapping his hands in what looked more like excitement than appreciation of Nox's climbing skills.

As I watched, Nox leaped out of the tree, and even though I knew he couldn't get hurt, fear lodged in my throat as he sailed toward the ground. Seconds before he'd have splatted on the ground, Silas grabbed him, whirling him around as Nox cheered.

Silas set him on the ground, and Nox grinned up at him, clearly having way too much fun. "That was awesome!"

"And it just about gave me a heart attack," I said, stepping into the clearing. Nox's eyes widened when he spotted me, and Silas reverted back to his human form, stepping back as if worried I'd hurt him as he hastily put on a mask he'd pulled out of his pocket. That made me tone down my annoyance, and I shot him a smile, hoping he'd know I meant him no harm.

"I'm glad you're doing better, Silas."

He nodded, dipping his head before turning to Nox. "You need to go now, right?"

"I do. But you have my number, so call me if you ever need me. Or if you just wanna play catch," he added with a wink, and Silas ducked his head, and I was pretty sure he was smiling.

Nox gave him a hug before stepping back and walking over to me, eyes bright as he asked, "Had a fun trip?"

"It was definitely something. I'll tell you when we get home."

"Let's go, then."

I took Nox's hand in mine, pressing a kiss to his knuckles, and magicked us home.

TWENTY-TWO

Nox

"We have some bad news," were the first words I heard as we stepped into the lounge, and I glared up at Harlan.

"See? This is what happens when you don't let me play with your pretty ass first thing in the morning!"

Harlan's cheeks turned red as he shook his head at me, turning my head so I was facing the others again.

"I'm sorry about him. I can't seem to find his off button," Harlan said, sounding truly apologetic, and Lionel laughed.

"Trust me, no one's been able to find it, and we've been trying far longer than you," he said, and I rolled my eyes.

"Ha ha, you're all hilarious. Now, if we're done with the 'mock Nox' part of our morning, can we get back to what the bad news is?"

"Well, it's news plural, to start with," Reece said with a grimace, and I threw my hands up in the air.

"Of course. Why wouldn't it be? Is it the kraken? Please tell me the kraken didn't lose it?" I demanded, crossing my fingers.

"It's not the kraken," Damien assured me, his arms resting on the back of the couch his mates sat on as he leaned forward, his mouth pressed in a firm line. I did not like that look on his face.

"It's the other two who lost it," Lionel added, and the relief I'd felt at the fact that the kraken was okay disappeared into thin air.

"The kelpie has already lured a few humans into the water, and we don't know if they're supposed to be food or future hosts. He's keeping them alive with his magic. For now," Zane said, and Maximus growled.

"Kym's been working non-stop for three days, and now this."

"I'm fine, Max. Channeling the others means I don't burn myself out doing it."

"Doesn't mean you don't still get exhausted," he argued, and Kym smiled up at him as if he was being especially cute.

"You know I have to do this. It's why I still have my magic. This is my purpose, Max."

Max sighed, and it sounded like they'd had this exact argument before. Wanting to nip it in the bud, I eyed Reece and asked, "You said plural. What's the other bad news?"

"The wyvern has been spotted in neighboring towns, attacking humans. That's how our scouts found him. He almost killed a man. The scouts who found him managed to alter the people's memories so they think a large eagle attacked them, but he needs to be stopped before he actually kills someone."

"The dark magic is getting stronger the longer it stays inside them," Harlan said, and I had to agree. And it worried me. Because the kraken was the most dangerous of them all, and if he lost control...

"Damien, I think you should let Kym channel you," I said, and he smiled faintly.

"I'd been intending to. We were just waiting on you. I've heard you're very good at forming a rapport with the supes, so I thought it'd be best if you joined us."

I blinked, surprised. I hadn't consciously been trying to form a rapport, like he'd said. I'd just wanted to make sure they were okay. Being around the Chasm for so long, I knew a thing or two about being affected by dark magic and feeling things you'd never feel otherwise. My sole intention had been to make sure Dell and Silas knew I understood they weren't the bad guys, that I saw them for who they were: kids who'd been dealt a really shitty hand.

"Where are we going first, then?" Harlan asked, probably sensing I was lost in my own thoughts.

"Chicago. We need to deal with the kelpie first, and free the humans he's trapped," Damien said. Turning to Lionel, he added, "Lionel, Zane, keep an eye on the kraken. The moment you sense something is wrong, or you see the dark magic spreading, you get us, okay? The wyvern can be distracted from his hunt, but if the kraken gets loose, it will be, well, hell."

Lionel and Zane both nodded, and after Zane had murmured a quiet goodbye to Wren, the two disappeared.

"Maximus, is your squad still guarding all three supes?" Damien asked, and Maximus nodded.

"I have four of my people at every location. The others are managing their duties between them."

"Great. If you need more people, borrow some from Zane's team."

"I will. I'll also keep my ear to the ground about any movements in the human realm that have anything to do with black magic."

"Good, do that. Reece, Arty, contact me if anything goes wrong. Have Caelan assist you wherever necessary."

"Go, Day. We'll be fine. I promise," Arty assured him, turning around to look up at him. They had one of their silent conversations, and I assumed Damien's hesitation had to do with the fact that the breakout at the Chasm had happened when he hadn't been here. Ever since that incident, he'd had a hard time leaving Otherworld, especially without his mates and Walker.

"All right, we better get going. Kym, Harlan, and Nox, you're with me. Everyone else, stay safe, okay?"

"We will, Damien," Mazia assured him, and Vaishnavi shot him a grin.

"Don't let that pretty face of yours get ruined," she called out, and Damien shook his head at her, before turning to us.

"Let's go."

I took Harlan's hand in mine as Damien's magic stirred around us, and then we were at the edge of a lake, the deep water a dangerous shade of dark green. All kinds of green slime floated on the surface, and while I'd enjoyed my dip in the Thames River the other day, I did not want to even dip my toes into this water. How was the kelpie living inside this lake? Or was it because of him that it was so dirty?

Harlan raised a brow at me, his lips tilted in a smirk. The bastard could read me too well already. "Ready for a dip, Trouble?"

I grumbled unintelligibly before glancing down at my clothes. We'd taken to wearing shirts every day since we had to visit the human realm so often, and I was wearing one of my favorites. I didn't want to ruin it in this muddy water.

I pulled it off, carefully placing it at the base of a nearby tree. When I turned back to him, Harlan's eyes were roaming all over my exposed torso, a heated look in his eyes.

"Do *not* give me a hard-on when we're about to face a fucking kelpie!" I growled, and the look dissipated as a chuckle slipped past his lips.

Then the jerk had the audacity to remove his own shirt. "Not helping!" I shouted, and leaped into the lake to save myself, instantly regretting it when strips of seaweed and green, yucky stuff started latching onto my skin.

"Urgh," I grumbled, shaking my arms to get rid of them as I swam deeper. Kym and Damien were already at the bottom, since neither of them gave a shit about getting their clothes dirty, facing off against the kelpie, who did not look happy.

I hadn't seen one before, not that I could remember, but I'd read about them, and this one looked quite similar to the ones in Damien's books. He had the body of a horse, but instead of legs, it was just a weird mashup of leathery skin that swayed gently in the water. It could easily be mistaken for smoke from a distance, but it definitely looked like skin. The color of his skin was a dark green that looked almost black; his eyes were green like the seaweed around him. I wondered what he looked like in human form, but it was a thought for later because the kelpie looked ready to attack. His ears were pinned back, his teeth flashing as he struck at the lakebed with a dark, smoking hoof.

"Can you put a ward around him, like the one you put around the kraken?" I asked Harlan, who'd caught up to me, and he nodded, swimming ahead.

I let him lead, watching as his spell wrapped around the kelpie, keeping him from escaping or using his magic to attack.

Unlike the kraken, he fought hard against the trap, kicking and striking against it repeatedly.

"Can you take him out of the water?" Kym called, and Harlan nodded. Damien waved him forward, and Harlan murmured another spell, making the trap—and the kelpie along with it—shoot up into the air.

I was about to follow them when my eyes fell on the two trapped humans. They were inside bubbles and seemed to be asleep. I swam closer, eyeing the bubbles they were inside. I was afraid to touch them, worried if the bubble burst they'd drown before I'd be able to help them. I'd need to come back for them once the kelpie was healed.

Decision made, I turned around and swam to the surface.

Harlan

I held on to the spell trapping the kelpie with all my might, his own magic almost too powerful for me. I hoped with Damien boosting him, Kym would be able to work quicker. I didn't think I'd be able to hold on for as long as the other healings had taken. To make things easier, I'd left the kelpie's lower body submerged so the water could support his weight, but it also gave him the support he needed to move around and slam against my ward.

Nox swam to the shore, and I spared a moment to glance at him, relief coursing through me. I'd been worried when he hadn't instantly followed us up, but of course he'd gotten distracted by something.

"Two humans below, in magic bubbles. You doing okay?"

I nodded, my eyes flicking back to the kelpie who kept slamming against my ward. I winced at a particularly forceful push, and Nox's eyes narrowed. He leapt back into the water and swam toward the kelpie.

Damien had taken to the air with Kym in his arms, his black wings beating against the pale blue sky as he hovered mid-air so Kym could drop fireballs on him. Nox expertly avoided them, staying at the edge of the ward as he closed in on the kelpie. Why was he such a risk taker? And why did I love him for it when it drove me crazy?

"Oi, Kelpie guy! Dude! Stop that. You'll break your head! Be a good horsey, okay?" Nox called, and I wasn't sure if it was the effect of Kym's fire, but the kelpie seemed to be listening to Nox, his pace slowing.

"That's right. You're a good horsey, aren't you? With your pretty green eyes and green skin," Nox cooed, and the kelpie stopped attacking the ward completely, his head tilted to the side as he watched Nox. His mane was caked with weeds, and it swung as he tilted his head this way and that, as if trying to figure out my crazy man.

"Such a sweet horsey. You don't want to hurt anyone, do you? You just want to be free of the pain. Don't worry. My friends are doing just that. Just be patient, okay?"

The kelpie squealed at the next strike of the fireball, and sympathy washed through me for the poor guy. I was sure that when he shifted, we'd find yet another person who hadn't deserved what happened to them. If I didn't already hate the queen of Underworld for what she did to Nox, I'd hate her for this.

It took another few minutes before the kelpie was fully healed, but I dropped my ward the moment he was, and he swam right up to Nox, gently headbutting him in the chest.

Nox ran his hand over the kelpie's head, smiling down at him. "Hey, buddy. Feeling better? How about we go down and get those humans before you shift back so we can tell you what's going on?"

The kelpie nickered, bowing his head low. Remorse shone in every line of his body, and I knew Nox could see it too.

"Hey, it's okay. You weren't yourself. Now, come on. Let's help those humans, yeah?"

The kelpie made a sound that was a mix of a yip and a neigh, and raced into the water, Nox following him with a laugh. I merely shook my head as Damien landed beside me with Kym in his arms. Kym's legs looked a little shaky as he straightened up, and he shook his head. "Once this is over, I'm never flying again. Ever."

Damien chuckled, running a hand through his hair. He'd shifted to his human form, probably so the kelpie wouldn't be too curious. He'd been too distracted to notice Damien before, but he would've definitely noticed now if he still had wings and horns.

"Was I that bad?" he asked Kym, and Kym's eyes widened before he shook his head.

"Not at all. I'm just sick of it."

"I feel you. I'm not a fan of heights," I said, and Kym gave me a small smile.

Nox and the kelpie returned before I could say anything, the human bubbles in tow. The bubbles arched out of the water and rested gently on solid ground before bursting, the humans inside slumping in the bushes. It was a man and a woman, both in their early twenties and clearly too young to be caught up in this shit.

"I'll take care of them," Damien said, already walking toward them, and I knew he'd erase their memories and make sure they got home safe.

I turned around as Nox swam to the shore, offering him a hand and pulling him up when he was close. The kelpie followed, though he stopped at the edge, looking into the water.

"Come on, won't you join us?" Nox asked, and the kelpie shook his head.

"I must stay," the kelpie said, and I was so startled that all I could do was stare at him.

"Did you just talk?" Nox demanded, never one to mince his words.

"I did," the kelpie agreed, his voice gravelly.

"Oh my god, I called you a good horsey. I'm so sorry!" Nox apologized, and I would've laughed if I wasn't still stunned.

Kym gave me a wide-eyed look, and I knew he was just as shocked as me.

"It helped," the kelpie said, swishing his mane to one side. It was the same dark green as his skin, but seaweed was tangled into the green hair, making it look like it was all weeds. "Thank you for destroying the black magic. I couldn't fight it."

"You knew what it was?" Nox asked, and the kelpie dipped his head.

"I've felt it before. Eaten it before," he added, his green eyes flickering away.

"Is there a reason you won't shift?" Nox asked, curiosity entering his tone.

"Been a long time since I did it. Like this form better," he explained, and Nox blinked, clearly stumped. He eyed the lake the kelpie swam in, and I knew he wanted to ask the kelpie to leave it. But he didn't.

"Can I ask your name?"

The kelpie bobbed his head, making the water around him splash. "I'm Alaric."

Nox smiled, kneeling down and patting Alaric's head. "It's nice to meet you, Alaric. I'll come by in a little while to check on you, okay?"

"Why would you do that?" he asked, honestly sounding puzzled.

Nox's smile widened, and he booped the kelpie on the nose. "Because you're a pretty horsey, and I want to be your friend. Is that okay?"

Bubbles appeared all over the lake and then drifted into the air, filling the sky with rainbow-colored bubbles. Nox laughed softly, as Alaric's answer was pretty clear.

"Awesome. Then I'll see you soon, my friend."

Alaric made that yip-neigh sound again and then disappeared under the water. Nox turned, the smile slipping from his face as he walked over to me.

I pulled him into a hug, and he buried his face in my neck, his body slumping against mine. "I want to murder Meredith."

My brows furrowed, and I pulled back to look at him. "Who?"

"The smoky witch in the Chasm. She isn't a queen of anything, so I'm going to call her Meredith now."

Of course he would. "Then I want to murder Meredith too. How about we do it together?"

"Deal."

TWENTY-THREE

Nox

"Kym, are you up to tackling the wyvern today? Or should we wait until tomorrow?"

Damien's question had me pulling out of Harlan's arms, and I looked over at Kym, who didn't look as tired as he usually did after a healing.

"We can do it today. Channeling you really helped. I don't feel as drained as I usually would at this point," Kym answered, and I was relieved. I wanted these supes freed as quickly as possible.

"That's great. The wyvern is up in the mountains of Nevada, and they're known to be great hunters, so we need to be careful in how we approach him. Wyverns are naturally wild, and with the dark magic affecting him, there's no telling what he can do," Damien said, and I felt eyes on me. I looked up to find Harlan staring at me.

"What?" I asked, and he shook his head.

"Just wondering if you'll end up getting in trouble," he said, and I narrowed my eyes at him.

"I haven't yet," I pointed out, and he sighed from the depths of his soul, sounding completely done with me.

"That's what worries me," he muttered, and I shook my head. I'd be fine, and then I'd show him I wasn't always reckless. I knew how to be careful. I did.

"Let's go. We can't afford to waste any time," Damien said, and I straightened up. Right, mission time.

Damien's magic stirred around us, and then we were in the high mountains, wind whipping around us and greenery surrounding us on all sides. Harlan's hand clamped on mine, tight as a vice, and I looked up at him. His eyes were wide, and he was staring at the drop a few feet from him.

I tugged him toward me, switching places so I was closer to the edge, and he gave me a grateful look. I popped a kiss to his chin in answer, and he smiled softly, squeezing my hand.

"Our scouts say the wyvern is in a cave around that bend," Damien said, pointing forward as he returned his phone to his pocket. I leaned forward to see if I could get a pick, but the bend was too sharp.

We followed Damien and Kym, and my skin started buzzing with excitement the closer we got. Wyverns were as rare as dragons, and while they were both equally powerful and knowledgeable, wyverns had never taken to humanity the way dragons had. Many dragons lived with the humans in their human form, but wyverns rarely did that, which was why they never passed through Otherworld. I didn't know if there was another realm where souls of animals and animal-like magical beings went, but if there was, that was probably where most wyverns went. But once a being had turned human, and experienced what it meant to be a human—the emotions, the needs, the greed, and all the little things—they belonged in the Otherworld after their life ended in the human realm.

A screech pierced the air just before we turned the corner, and Damien pulled Kym against him to keep him safe as the wyvern came flying at warp speed, clearly having sensed us.

He aimed straight for me, as if knowing I wanted to play with him. Harlan's hand tightened around mine, and I had no doubt the wyvern could carry us both, but unlike me, Harlan wasn't a fan of heights.

Which was why I jerked my hand out of his a moment before the wyvern reached us, his claws clamping onto my shoulder. He didn't even pause; that's how smooth he was. He just picked me up mid-flight, and off we went.

"I'll be okay!" I called to Harlan, who was staring at us with wide eyes as Kym and Damien hurried to his side.

I looked up at the wyvern, and all I could see was his slate-gray underbelly, and his long tail that flicked this way and that, helping him change directions as he flew.

"Hey, Mr. Wyvern!" I called, figuring I might as well make conversation. What else was there to do? "My friends want to help, you know. The dark magic is hurting you, and we want to heal you. Don't you want to be free of it?"

The wyvern didn't seem to be hearing me, probably because of how fucking fast he flew. He was faster than the roller coaster in the amusement park Harlan had taken me to, and that shit had been *fast*.

If I was human, I was sure I'd be a sniffling mess, or dead. But even now, I could feel his claws digging into my skin, and while they wouldn't have hurt me in a different situation, right now they were drenched in dark magic, and that hurt.

I gave an ooof as the wyvern unceremoniously dropped me onto a large rocky surface, dropping to his two feet in front of me. His yellow, reptilian eyes flashed as he walked over to me, his head coming way too close to my face as he sniffed me. I stayed still, returning the favor as I examined him from head to toe.

He was huge, almost as big as my living room, with yellow eyes, slate-gray leathery skin, and wicked claws on his feet. His tail was easily six feet long, and one swipe of it would be more than enough to knock a grown man out.

The black magic was clearly affecting him badly. He had drool leaking out of his mouth, and his eyes kept flicking everywhere, his body coiled with tension. It almost looked like he was anxious.

"Hey," I murmured softly and his eyes slid back to me. He sniffed at me, and I made a face as some of his drool soaked into the shirt I'd put on before we left the lake. Oh no, please don't let it be ruined.

"Hey, wyvern guy. Don't be scared, okay? You'll feel better soon," I murmured. Where the hell were the others? Hadn't Damien followed the wyvern?

The wyvern screeched again, making my ears ring since he hadn't given me the courtesy of moving his head away before he did it.

"Hey, hey, you'll be fine. I promise," I murmured, and his eyes turned back to me, narrowing slightly as he watched me.

Before I could react, he swiped a claw at me, tearing a large gash on my arm. I curled up as pain lanced through me, the dark magic burning through the wound and reminding me of my stint in the Burning Chasm.

I stared at him through bleary eyes, bracing myself as his claw came at me again.

It never hit me because a shield of blue magic was suddenly between us, and I watched as Harlan dropped beside me, his eyes on the wyvern as he finished his spell, trapping the wyvern in his ever-useful ward.

My white knight had come to my rescue. Again.

Harlan

My skin still felt itchy and weird from the flight, and it wasn't something I ever wanted to try again. But I was grateful I'd asked Damien to carry me too, because otherwise I might not have been able to stop the wyvern in time.

As soon as the spell was finished, I hurried to Nox's side, falling to my knees as I pulled him toward me. The gash on his arm was deep, showing hints of bone. A distant part of me wondered how a body made of magic could look so real, but my focus was on making sure Nox didn't bleed out. Could he *die* from bleeding out?

"I'm okay," Nox assured me, and I rolled my eyes at him as I pulled my shirt off, tearing off a strip as I muttered a healing spell. I wasn't as good at healing spells as my sister, Rhiannon, but I knew enough to do some basic first aid.

"Sure, sure. You're just fine. Just like you weren't completely reckless back there. Why did you pull away, Nox?" I demanded as I wrapped his arm. I could hear Damien and Kym behind me, tackling the wyvern. I trusted my ward to hold for now, but I kept half my attention on it, not willing to risk my teammates just because my mate didn't know how to work with one.

"I knew he would've grabbed me, and I didn't want you to tag along. You hate heights," he explained, as if it made perfect sense. To him, maybe it did.

"I could've—hell, I *would've* shielded us, Nox. That's what I was going to do, but you pulled away before I could complete the spell."

"Oh," he mumbled, a sheepish look on his face.

"Yeah, oh. I need you to trust me, Nox. We're partners. We should work together. You can't always do things that you think are best for me without my input. Relationships don't work like that," I said, my voice soft. I knew he'd had my best interests at heart, but I needed him to understand how much it scared me whenever he did something reckless like what he'd done today.

"I'm sorry," Nox said, looking truly apologetic as he met my eyes, his gray ones shining. "I guess I'm just so used to doing everything on my own. I'll try to be better, I promise."

I cupped his face with my palm, the one not coated in his blood, and smiled. "I don't want you to change, Trouble. I like that you're a little troublesome, that you take risks. You make me not want to be so cautious all the time, and after a lifetime of being too careful, I really need that. I just want you to remember that you're not alone. You have me in your corner now, and I'll always be there for you. I love you, Trouble, and that means I love all your craziness too, even if it scares me most of the time."

Nox laughed softly, wincing as he struggled to sit up. I helped him up, and he smiled brightly, his eyes twinkling. "I love you too. And I know that no matter how reckless I am, I'll always have my white knight coming to my rescue."

"Always," I promised, pressing a kiss to his lips.

"If you're both done being sickening, can we get some help here?" Kym called, and I pulled away with a grimace, turning around as I felt a tug at the spell keeping the ward in place.

I got to my feet, pushing more magic into the spell as I walked closer to the ward, Nox close at my heels. "Sorry, sorry!"

I held the ward as Kym dropped more fireballs onto the wyvern, who was slamming his tail again and again into my ward, determined to break it.

I could see Kym was starting to flag even with Damien's magic boosting him, and I hoped the wyvern would heal soon. I did not want to deal with him another day.

"Come on, heal already," I heard Kym mutter, and I stared at the wyvern hard, down to his soul so I could see how much work we had left. There were still dark spots on his soul, the black inkiness of them clinging to his soul.

An idea struck me, and while I wasn't sure if it'd work, I was willing to try anything at this point, and I was sure the others would agree.

"What if he was on his back? I think his hard skin is somehow keeping the fire from affecting him fully," I called out, and Kym gave me a thumbs-up, his brows furrowed in concentration.

I used a binding spell to tie the wyvern's legs together, jerking hard so he fell onto his back. It had the added benefit of stopping his tail-attack on my ward, and Kym pounced on the opportunity, dropping fireballs one after the other on his exposed belly.

I dropped the ward so Kym could get closer to the wyvern and attack more easily, but the moment the ward disappeared, there was a flash of light, and the wyvern transformed into a...cat. The cat's yellow eyes flashed at me as it slipped through my wards, racing into the rocks.

"Fuck!" I growled as my spell dissipated with nothing to hold on to. If the wyvern had been in his right mind, I was sure he'd have disappeared. But since he had dark magic coursing through him, urging him to be wild and hunt, he shifted back into his wyvern form a few feet away from us.

He shot into the sky before I could trap him again, letting out a screech as he flew up in a straight line before diving back toward us, aiming straight for Damien and Kym.

"Shit!" Nox cursed, and I hushed him as I murmured a spell, raising my palm up. A shield fell between the wyvern and Damien a moment before he slammed into it, and Damien took off in the other direction as the wyvern recovered.

I turned to Nox, who had his lower lip gripped between his teeth, his eyes wide as they followed the wyvern. Worry shot through me as I realized the cloth I'd wrapped around his wound was soaked with blood, but I didn't have the chance to do anything more as the wyvern changed course and aimed for us.

"Trust me," I murmured, and Nox's uninjured hand fell to my shoulder.

"I do."

I modified the ward spell to keep the dark magic out and arched my arm over us, covering us with it. The wyvern, clearly learning from his mistake, banked left just before he could slam into the ward, screeching angrily as he flew around us.

"I need a couple of minutes to make a strong enough ward to hold him," I muttered, and Nox squeezed my shoulder.

"Damien!" Nox shouted, and Damien glanced at us from where he hovered mid-air, Kym looking very unhappy in his arms, his skin a pallid shade. "Distract him!"

I was pretty sure I heard Kym whimper, but Damien nodded, glancing down at Kym before shaking his head and flying toward us. He dropped Kym inside the ward, where he high-tailed it to Nox's side, carefully touching his wound, making sure any dark magic hadn't snuck into Nox. I was relieved when he didn't use his fire on Nox, telling me he was safe from the dark magic, at least.

Turning my focus to the wyvern, I watched as Damien used his magic to summon a bow and arrow out of thin air, shooting one at the wyvern's wing as he flew toward him. The arrow must've been imbued with Damien's magic because it made the wyvern stumble, even if he didn't completely stop.

The wyvern kept coming toward Damien, no matter how many arrows he shot at him. It was hard to get a trap around a moving object, and I realized I'd have to ask Damien to put himself in danger. I was so glad his mates weren't here.

"Damien! I need you to engage him! Get him to stay in one place!" I called, and Damien nodded, his eyes still on the wyvern.

I watched as the bow and arrow disappeared, and Damien flew toward the wyvern, circling him as he drew closer, confusing the wyvern as he turned this way and that to keep Damien in his line of sight.

I started the spell, my eyes tracking the wyvern as I wound the ward around him. I had to put Damien inside it too since he was so close, but he'd be able to fly out once it'd closed.

Just as the ward closed, the wyvern swiped his tail at Damien, knocking him out of the ward. Knowing how powerful the wyvern's tail was, I knew Damien wouldn't be able to catch himself in time, and he was headed straight for the rocky edge of the mountains.

I couldn't focus on another spell while still holding onto this one, but I didn't have to. There was a sudden burst of magic, and suddenly, a large, snakelike dragon appeared from thin air, catching Damien on its back before he could slam into the rocks.

"Ro'Shassz!" Nox breathed behind me, and I gaped at the snake-dragon. This was Ro'Shassz? The lazy snake that always hung around Walker's neck? How did he even get here? I'd known he had magic of his own—or rather he had some of Damien's magic—but I hadn't realized he could do...*this*.

The snake-dragon was black, with shiny scales covering his sides and long, slate-gray horns sticking out of his head. His green eyes were narrowed as he slithered through the air toward us, Damien on his back. Green smoke escaped his mouth as he hissed, and he dropped Damien off beside us before turning to the wyvern.

"Need any help with the bird?" he asked, clearly addressing Damien.

Damien huffed in amusement, shaking his head. "Nah, we'll be fine. Right, Harlan?"

I nodded quickly, tightening my grip on the ward reflexively. But it seemed even the wyvern was in shock of the flying snake-dragon.

"You can go, Ro. Thanks for the save. And don't tell Reece and Arty about this," he added, and Ro'Shassz hissed in a way that made me think he was laughing.

"Oh, I'll be sure to tell them all about it." He disappeared before Damien could protest, and he groaned, rubbing a palm over his face.

Shaking his head, he glanced at the wyvern, who was eyeing us curiously, his eyes looking clearer. Had the shock of seeing Ro'Shassz cleared his head of the dark magic's control?

Whatever it was, he didn't react as Damien took to the skies with Kym in his arms, who seemed to have recovered from his bout of nausea. The two hovered over the wyvern as Kym started pelting him with his fire, and the wyvern merely stood there, making small painful sounds every once in a while that he seemed to be actively suppressing.

It was a long few minutes before the dark magic had fully burned out of him, and I waited for Damien and Kym to drop down beside us before removing the ward around the wyvern.

I kept a spell ready on my lips, magic buzzing beneath my fingertips just in case the wyvern reacted unfavorably.

When the wyvern just sat and watched us with his yellow, reptilian eyes for a whole minute, Nox hurried over to him like I'd known he would, and I wondered if the wyvern would stay in this form too, like the kelpie had.

But the moment Nox was close enough, he shifted into a dark-haired man, his clothes a mirror of what I wore. Was he unaware of human fashion, or did he just like my clothes? I wasn't going to ask.

"I apologize for harming you. I…I wasn't myself," he said, his voice deep and almost guttural.

"It's okay. I understand. Are you feeling better now?" Nox asked, and the wyvern nodded his head, his eyes flicking around.

"Thank you for helping me," he said, and Nox smiled.

"It's our job. We've also made sure none of the villagers remember you, so you'll be safe here," he said, and the wyvern blinked, surprised.

"Oh, thank you. May I know your name?" he asked, stepping forward. I found myself stepping closer to Nox. I knew the wyvern wouldn't hurt him now, but it was hard to get my instincts on the same track.

"I'm Nox, and this is my mate, Harlan," Nox introduced, leaning around me since I'd pretty much stepped between them.

The wyvern looked up at me, his yellow, reptilian eyes eerie in his human form. "I mean him no harm. I promise."

To Nox, he said, "I'm Lancelot. This isn't my home, but I might stay here for a while. I assure you I won't hurt the villagers, or anyone else."

"I know you won't. What happened wasn't your fault." Nox proceeded to explain everything, just like he had with everyone else, and Lancelot listened carefully. He seemed to take it better than the others, and when Nox was done, he merely nodded thoughtfully and thanked us again.

Damien glanced at his phone, and then at Kym, who looked dead on his feet, and declared, "We should get going."

"Yeah," Nox agreed, turning to Lancelot. "Do you have a phone?"

"A phone?" Lancelot asked, sounding puzzled, and I wondered how long it'd been since he'd interacted with humans.

"Uh, never mind. If you plan on staying in this area, I'll visit you sometime, if that's okay with you?" Nox asked, and Lancelot eyed him suspiciously.

"You don't believe I will behave, do you?"

"It's not that. I promise. I just want to make sure you're okay."

Lancelot blinked, as if he hadn't expected that, but then he nodded. Nox gave him one last smile before taking my hand and turning to Damien, ready to head back.

Tomorrow, we'd heal the kraken, and then finally, it'd be over, at least for a short time until we figured out how to destroy the queen—*Meredith*.

TWENTY-FOUR

Nox

When we got back to Otherworld, Harlan dragged me to Reece, and I didn't fight him. I knew I'd scared him earlier, and I regretted it immensely. I'd only been thinking about keeping Harlan safe, but I should've remembered he could take care of himself. Like he'd said, I should've trusted him.

It didn't take Reece long to heal me as Damien updated him about everything that had happened as he ran around the room with Walker on his shoulders. Walker was busy giggling and talking to Ro'Shassz, who kept sticking his tail in Damien's face to annoy him and make Walker laugh, so I doubted he'd heard any of what Damien had said.

When Reece declared I was all healed up, I wished them a good night and dragged Harlan back to our cabin, intent on making things right with him.

"I'm sorry," I said the moment we were inside, and he raised a brow at me as he closed the door.

"What for?"

"Earlier. For not trusting you. For scaring you."

Harlan smiled softly and placed his palms on my waist, tugging me closer. I tipped my head up so I could see him better, and he wrapped an arm around me before cupping my face with his other hand. "I know you are, Trouble. And it's okay. I understand how hard it is for you. You've depended only on yourself for a long time, and it's hard to stop doing that. I just need you to remember you're not alone now, okay?"

"I'll do better. I promise," I murmured, and Harlan ran his thumb over my lower lip. I took the opportunity to take his thumb into my mouth, sucking on it with my eyes trained on his. The blue of his eyes darkened with desire, his pupils flaring as I nipped at the pad of his thumb.

He pulled it away, replacing it with his mouth as he pulled me into a deep, heady kiss. His tongue slipped into my mouth, tangling with mine as he tasted me. I moaned into his mouth as his palm slid down my back to rest on my ass with his other one, squeezing slightly so my erection was pressed against his thigh. I could feel his hardness against my abdomen, and I pressed closer, rocking into the contact.

Harlan groaned and pulled away, taking my hand and dragging me to our bedroom. He worked at my clothes, quickly getting me out of them and throwing them carelessly onto the floor, something he rarely did.

He removed his own clothes at warp speed as I stood there admiring the view, and once he was naked, he grabbed me by the waist and threw me onto the mattress, making me laugh.

My laughter dissolved into a moan as he covered me with his larger body and pulled me into another intense kiss. No one had ever kissed me the way Harlan did, as if it was the first and last time he'd ever get to kiss me. He put his all in it, and I could feel his love and care in every swipe of his tongue, in every brush of our lips, in every little nip on my skin. I hoped he could feel how much I loved him too.

He pushed my hair away from my face as he pulled away, his eyes meeting mine for a moment before he dipped down to bite my jaw, the pain making me gasp and moan breathily. He trailed bites and kisses down my body, giving extra attention to my nipples. I hadn't known nipple play turned me on, but apparently, I was very much a nipple man.

When Harlan finally reached my groin, I was a mess. My cock was leaking precum like a faucet, and my lips were swollen. I bet I made a sexy picture, and from the look on Harlan's face as he examined me head to toe, he agreed with my assessment.

I stretched my arms above my head to give him a better look, and he shook his head, a small smile playing at his lips.

"Such a brat," he murmured softly as he settled between my thighs and wrapped his lips around the tip of my cock. I resisted the urge to push up into the warm heat of his mouth, grabbing onto the headboard to keep myself still.

Harlan used one hand to jerk me off as his tongue teased my tip, his other hand massaging my balls in a way that made me feel I'd just about reached heaven. It was hard to believe I was the only guy Harlan had been with because he was such a natural. Then again, I thought everything about him was sexy, so who knew? Maybe it was just a he's-my-mate side-effect.

"Fuck, Harlan," I gasped as he removed his hand and slid my cock deeper into his mouth. The wet heat of his mouth felt wonderful, and it took all my focus to stop myself from thrusting my hips up.

I let him set the pace, whimpering softly—a sound I'd never admit to making—when his finger traced around my hole. I was so close I didn't think I'd even need him to get his finger inside me.

I was proven right when my orgasm showed up out of nowhere, crashing into me with the power of a thousand spells, making stars appear behind my eyelids as I cried out Harlan's name.

He drank me down, swallowing every last drop of my cum as I shuddered through the aftershocks, my body feeling limp and relaxed. I didn't think I'd move for a few hours.

The sound of jerking off reached my ears, and I forced my eyes open to see Harlan leaning over me, his hand working at his straining dick, his eyes on me. I licked my lips, and he leaned down to kiss them, his speed increasing.

Warm cum splashed onto my stomach as he came, and he kept up the punishing pace, murmuring my name in my ear as he came. When he was done, he slumped over me, exhausted, and I wrapped my arms around him, squishing his cum between us. I didn't care, though, because all I needed in that moment was to hold him and keep him close.

"I'll get a cloth," Harlan mumbled, pulling back, but I didn't let him get too far.

"Use my shirt," I told him, not caring in the least that it was one of my favorites.

Harlan did, though, because he grabbed his own shirt instead, using it to wipe us clean before throwing it back onto the floor.

I snuggled into him, sighing happily as he wrapped his arms around me, cocooning me into his warmth. And even though it would get too warm in a little bit like it did every night, I knew I wouldn't want to pull away simply because it was Harlan. Fuck, I'd turned into a cheesy sap like Zane. *No one must know.*

Harlan

"What do you think will happen once the kraken is healed?" Nox asked. Some people fell asleep right after sex. Nox wasn't one of those people.

"I guess it depends on what Meredith would do next. Unless Damien plans to take the fight to her."

"She knows the Chasm way better than us. It doesn't make sense to go into her territory, not when we don't know exactly how powerful she is down there," Nox mused, and I had to agree.

"What about the King of Afterworld? Didn't Damien say something about him earlier when Reece was healing you?" I asked, and Nox's brows furrowed as he thought about it.

"Oh, yeah. He said Tharion would be coming here tomorrow. He's going to check out the ward, see if his magic can strengthen it further. And then Tharion and Damien will probably plan how they're going to get rid of Meredith."

I hadn't seen the king of Afterworld yet, or his sibling, Fate, at least not here. But I'd heard quite a lot about both of them, and I'd met Fate in Mistvale as Celeste, though I obviously hadn't known they also moonlight as Fate.

"Tomorrow, huh? Let's hope we can deal with the kraken quickly, then," I said, squeezing Nox closer to me as he hummed.

"Zane texted me earlier. They said the kraken was pretty mellow the whole day, and the dark magic on him didn't grow at all. Instead, Zane's sure it's decreasing."

I blinked at that, taking a moment to absorb that information. "So, the kraken is healing himself?"

"Seems like it. He seemed really old, older than the others. Maybe that gives him more power?"

"It's possible. I'm glad he can fight it then because I'm not sure we could've fought him if he'd succumbed to the dark magic," I murmured. We would've still tried, but our chances of winning would've been very low indeed.

"Yeah, I do not want to be fighting that guy. I would like to make friends, though," Nox mused, and I chuckled. Of course he would.

"Come on, now. We should sleep if you want to be up early tomorrow. I'm guessing Kym and Damien would want to get it over with as soon as possible," I said, and Nox sighed softly.

"You're right. I don't know why we don't need food but still need sleep. It's not fair," Nox muttered, and I smiled. He could be such a child sometimes.

"Well, I don't know about you, but sleeping helps me refill my magical well, so to speak. And it clears my mind, too."

"My mind is always buzzing, though I guess not when I'm sleeping. Huh, I guess sleep is good for something," he murmured, and I smiled, unable to resist placing a kiss on his forehead.

"How about this? You sleep now, and if all goes well tomorrow, we'll go on a date at the earliest possible time," I offered, and his eyes lit up.

"A date? That could be fun. Where are you taking me?"

"I haven't thought about it yet, but it'll be someplace good, I promise. But first, sleep."

"Fine, fine. Will you sing me a lullaby?" he asked with a cheeky grin, and I shook my head.

"Brat. Close your eyes, come on."

Nox did what I'd asked somewhat reluctantly, and I wrapped my arm around him, curling him into my arms. We'd get too hot in a while, but Nox never seemed to mind, so I held on to him.

After a few minutes, he relaxed in my arms, sleeping peacefully, and I smiled down at him. With my free hand, I pushed his hair away from his face, tucking the stray strands behind his ear.

I'd made him go to sleep, but I was finding it hard to follow him. While I'd assured him I was okay with what had happened today, it'd really shaken me.

I was a tad bit overprotective of the people I cared about, and I'd be the first one to admit it. In the human realm, it'd been a necessity because of the way warlocks were hunted through centuries. But here, I was having a hard time reconciling the fact that I wouldn't lose Nox even if he were to get mortally wounded.

The panic I'd felt today was something I'd only experienced twice before, and even those times had been faint imitations of what I'd felt today. When my sister had been attacked by a shifter she'd been dating, I'd been more angry than scared, even though she'd been badly hurt. And when my best friend was attacked by Cynthia, the witch working for Meredith, I'd felt panic unlike anything I'd experienced before then.

Both those times felt like nothing compared to what I'd felt today, and I knew it was something I needed to deal with myself. It was my issue, and all I could do was tell myself again and again that Nox would be okay until my brain decided to accept it.

Nox mumbled in his sleep, and I buried my face in his hair, breathing him in to center myself. Nox was here, and he was safe. As long as he had me, he'd always be safe. I'd make sure of it.

TWENTY-FIVE

Nox

The scene we walked into when we stepped into the lounge the next day was so reminiscent of yesterday that I jerked to a halt and glanced up at Harlan, my eyes wide.

"Did we somehow go back in time?" I demanded, and Harlan smirked as his eyes took in the room.

"It looks like it. Please don't tell me we have more bad news," Harlan asked, giving Reece a pleading look. The face Reece made was not promising, and I found myself crossing the fingers of my free hand, the other tightening around Harlan's.

"Well, we have news. Whether it's good or bad is up for debate," Reece said, and I groaned.

"Somebody spit it out, please," I begged, and Zane took pity on me. I knew I liked them for a reason.

"The kraken isn't in the ward anymore," they said, and Harlan's hand jerked in mine.

"What? But I'd made sure the ward was as powerful as it could be. It was meant to keep every last speck of dark magic inside," Harlan protested, and Zane gave him a tight-lipped smile.

"Exactly. But this morning, there was no dark magic left in the kraken. Or at least, that's what I saw. Some of Max's scouts are still tailing the kraken, and I think he knows it, but he hasn't attacked them. Somehow, he can sense they don't mean him harm. Either way, it seems like he healed himself all on his own," Zane explained, and I whistled softly. That was some mad magic the kraken had. He could create a lot of trouble with it if he so wished, but it was clear to me he just wanted a quiet life.

"I want to talk to him," I decided, and Harlan sighed.

"How did I know you were going to say that?" he demanded, and I grinned up at him.

"Because you know me and love me and will do anything for me," I replied, and he shook his head.

"Lord knows why, but I will," he muttered, and I felt all warm and fluttery for a second. That was until Zane opened their mouth.

"Oh, look who's all cheesy now. I guess that answers your question, Nox." I didn't need to think too long to recall what they were referring to, remembering the day I'd asked them if I'd turn that sappy too once I found my mate.

Not willing to admit that I had, in fact, turned into a sap filled mess, I stuck my tongue out at them as Harlan's phone pinged.

"That's where they're at," Maximus said, and I realized that while I was verbally sparring with Zane, Harlan had taken to figuring out where the kraken was. For me. Man, I loved this guy.

"Is there anything we need to do after we've met with the kraken?" Harlan asked the room at large, and everyone shook their heads.

"Tharion will be here this evening, and we're doing an informal meeting of sorts to get him up to speed, so just be here for that," Damien said, and Harlan nodded, his eyes flicking to mine.

Without him saying a word, I knew what he wanted to say: Date time!

Hell yes. After all that monster-wrangling, I deserved some alone time with my mate. Especially because I had no clue when the next metaphorical bomb would drop, and I wanted to savor every quiet moment we got.

But before we could go on the date, we had a very special supe to meet.

Harlan offered me his hand, which I seemed to have let go of at some point, and I took it instantly. I waved at the room as his magic stirred around us, and then we were near the Thames River, much further from the spot where we'd first trapped the kraken.

Since this water wasn't as bad as the kelpie's lake, I dived into it without a second thought, Harlan close behind me. We swam deeper and deeper into the river, almost reaching its base before we finally spotted the kraken. He was a few feet in front of us, but he turned when we showed up, sensing our approach.

Harlan

"Hello! I'm glad to see you're doing better. I'm Nox, and this is Harlan. We're sorry about trapping you earlier," Nox said, twitching forward a little with every word he spoke.

The kraken turned around fully so he was facing us, and I swallowed as I took in his whole form. He was larger than an SUV, with tentacles almost ten feet long, and he had eight of them, though some were smaller than the others.

One of his tentacles reached out for Nox, and I tensed, ready to put myself between them. But the kraken merely brushed Nox's arm before pulling away, and I relaxed a little.

"There is no need to apologize, Nox. I understand it was only to keep the humans safe. I couldn't trust the black magic inside me, and I did not expect you to. It is your duty to protect the humans, and so you did."

"My duty?" Nox asked curiously, and the kraken waved a tentacle at both of us.

"You are both Otherworlders, are you not?" the kraken asked, and I shared a wide-eyed look with Nox. No one in the human realm was supposed to know about Otherworld. Right?

"How do you know about Otherworld?" Nox asked, swimming even closer to the kraken. I followed him, grabbing his hand so I could jerk him away if something went wrong.

"I've been alive a long time. I was asleep for a while, but before I went to sleep, everyone knew about the Otherworlders. It's how all the old legends came to be," the kraken said, and Nox hummed softly.

"Can I ask your name?" he asked finally, and the kraken bowed his head slightly, which mostly looked like him rolling forward in the water a little.

"I'm Ebenezer. You can call me Eben," he said, and Nox smiled.

"Okay, Eben. I just wanted to check in with you, see you were okay, after we heard you'd healed yourself. If you ever need a place to stay or anything, please visit the Mistvale town.

It's watched over by a storm dragon, and a really safe place for all kinds of supes," Nox said, and I realized he hadn't mentioned it to Alaric or Lancelot. Maybe because it was obvious they were determined to stay where they'd been?

"I'm not usually welcome in places humans reside in, but I shall keep it in mind. Thank you for coming to see me," Ebenezer said, and Nox smiled.

"It was my pleasure."

Eben turned around then, resuming his journey to wherever he was headed. Nox turned to me, a curious look in his eyes. "How old do you think he is? The dragon of Mistvale is like 2000 years old, right? And he doesn't know about us."

"So Eben must be older," I finished for him, and he nodded rapidly, eyes wide.

"That is one ancient man. It makes me sad that he's still alone," he said, his face softening.

"Are you going to talk to Fate about him too?" I asked, and Nox gave me a dry look.

"I'm going to talk to them about all five of the supes. Tonight," he said, and I smiled. Of course he was. "But first, date time. What are we doing?"

"Whatever you want," I offered, crossing my fingers and hoping he didn't pick something too crazy.

"Anything I want?" he asked brightly, which only increased my anxiety. But since I was a good mate who loved him to pieces, I just nodded. "Awesome! I want to go shopping."

"Shopping?" I asked, confused.

"Uh, more like I just want to go into a clothing store and try out a bunch of stuff. Usually, I just show Reece what kind of clothes I want, and he magicks them up. But I want to do it the normal way once. We won't actually buy anything, but you can maybe take pictures of me wearing them to show Reece?

It's a stupid idea, isn't it?" I pressed my palm to his lips to stop his rambling, shaking my head.

"Stop that," I said. "It's a great idea. Let's do this."

Nox grinned at me, his eyes lighting up. "You sure? You won't get bored?"

"Get bored watching you strut around in gorgeous outfits? Not likely," I said, and he chuckled.

"Come on, then. Before we become a part of the river," Nox said, and I blinked. I'd almost forgotten we were still in the water.

I followed Nox out of the water, using a spell to dry us so we wouldn't have to return to Otherworld for a change of clothes, for which Nox gave me a deep, sexy thank-you kiss.

We decided to visit a store right there in London since Nox wasn't looking for a particular store, and when he spotted one he liked the displays of, we went inside.

Nox beelined for the rack of floaty shirts in bright colors, and I followed him in, nodding at the saleswoman who greeted us. Nox had blown right past her, but now he walked back to greet her and tell her the clothes looked great.

I spent the next couple of hours watching Nox pick through the selections and then try on each outfit. As promised, I got to see him strut around in them, and I did my duty of taking a ton of pictures.

"You know, I could take one of these outfits," Nox mused, looking at all the clothes he'd tried on. "Or maybe more."

The mischief on his face had me thinking I wouldn't like whatever he was planning. "Oh yeah? And how's that?"

"Well, I could just take them all into the trial room, ask you to come in to help me with something, and then we just magick back to Otherworld with all the clothes. It was what we used to do before Reece got the magic and figured out how it worked."

That was news to me. I'd just assumed Damien did that before Reece, but then Damien must've had other, more important duties than making clothes for his people.

"So, does Reece make clothes for all of Otherworld?" I asked, and Nox shook his head.

"Just for the inner circle, more or less. Unless someone needs some type of specific clothes that you wouldn't find here. Like something with a hole for a tail," Nox explained, and I nodded. That made more sense, since there were a lot of people in Otherworld.

"Well, if the others do it too, I guess it isn't that big of a deal," I reasoned, and Nox grinned widely, knowing he had me.

"Exactly. And humans are very adept at making sense of things. They'll make themselves believe we weren't here at all, or something similar," he said, and I wondered how humans could be so oblivious. Or did they intentionally ignore the unexplainable because it scared them?

"Let's steal some clothes, then," I said, and Nox chuckled.

"You look so excited about the prospect," he teased, and I shook my head, smirking at him.

"Mischief is your thing, Trouble. I'm all about being cautious."

"Sometimes, some mischief can be exactly what you need," he said, and I smiled, looking into his eyes.

"Yeah, I know that now."

Nox smiled happily, grabbing my hand and dragging me into the changing room, intent on completing his heist.

Once he'd closed the trial room's door, packing us in the narrow space, I pressed him against the wall and claimed his lips, kissing him deeply as I wrapped an arm around his waist. He hummed in my mouth as he kissed me back, and in that moment, I couldn't imagine being happier than I was right then.

Otherworld was safe for now. We had reinforcements coming in in the form of the king of Afterworld, and we were going to figure out a game plan to defeat Meredith. All the infected supes were healed and safe.

And above all else, I had my mate in my arms, safe and sound. How could I not be happy?

TWENTY-SIX

Harlan

When we got back to Otherworld, King Tharion still hadn't arrived, so we went back to our cabin, where Nox spent a while rearranging his closet with all his new outfits. I had fun just watching him enjoy himself, and once he was done, we had some cuddle time where things might've gotten a bit more handsy than we'd intended.

"How about—" I started before Nox cut me off with a kiss. I groaned into his mouth as he climbed on top of me, and I wanted to give in. Fuck, did I want it. But I also knew that if we got side-tracked now, we'd end up being late for the meeting, and I knew Nox didn't want that either.

"How about we go for a walk?" I asked, keeping Nox from kissing me again so I could get the full question out.

He made a face like I'd said something that made no sense. "A walk? Seriously?"

"Do you really want to be late for the meeting?" I asked, raising a brow, and he huffed.

"I don't. But we can squeeze in a quickie, can't we?" he asked with a pout, making me smile.

"Afterward, I'll sex you up as much as you want. How does that sound?"

Nox narrowed his eyes at me, gauging me to see if I was serious. "You promise?"

"You have my word," I assured him with a smile, and he smirked.

"Okay, my knight. We have a deal." He hopped to his feet, offering me his hand. I took it, letting him pull me up.

We headed out of the cabin, deciding to take a leisurely walk toward the villa so we could check in with everyone before King Tharion arrived.

Nox's eyes fell on the Burning Chasm as we walked past the ward surrounding it, and he had a thoughtful look on his face.

"What are you thinking about?" I asked, and he turned to me, a crease between his brows.

"Just everything that has happened recently. I'd been conflicted about it before, but I'm sure now. I don't want to go back to being the Keeper. If your ward idea works out, great. If not, I'll ask Damien to hire someone else, but I'll tell him to set up a team of people instead of just putting it all on one person."

I smiled, squeezing his hand. I knew the job had been important to him at one point, but I was glad he saw now how draining it'd been for him. Of course, I hadn't been here when he'd been the Keeper, but I'd heard enough about that time from him and the others to have a pretty solid idea of what it'd been like for him.

"I think that's a great plan. You can join me in Max's squad and we can continue to fight evil together," I said, and he grinned at me, his eyes sparkling.

"That sounds absolutely perfect."

His eyes strayed back to the Chasm, but the crease between his brows had disappeared, telling me he was thinking about something else entirely now.

"What do you think her next step would be?" Nox mused, and I knew without asking he meant Meredith.

"I honestly don't know. If she tries to break out, she'd still be stuck inside the ward, though I'm hoping she doesn't know that and tries it anyway. It'd be fun to see her struggle."

"I can't argue with that. How big is the ward around the Chasm? You said you built it in a spherical shape, right?"

"Yep. It goes around seventy feet deep, forty feet on the sides, and as tall above ground as the Chasm. They're not escaping, trust me," I assured him, and he nodded.

"There you are! When will you start keeping your phone on you?" Lionel demanded as he landed beside us. "Zane texted. King Tharion is here, and we've been summoned. Damien thought you should explain the infected souls' situation since you talked to them all."

"I do have my phone. I just accidentally put it on silent," Nox said, eyes on the phone he'd pulled out of his pocket.

Lionel shook his head, muttering unintelligibly. I just smiled at my mate as he threw an arm around the man, glad to have him in my life. Or second life.

Until a few weeks ago, I couldn't have imagined this was where Fate would lead me. Death had always seemed like such a permanent, scary thing, but it had led me to the most precious person to me.

Nox was reckless, crazy, and scared the shit out of me. But he was also sweet and had the biggest heart I'd ever come across. I was lucky to have him and the chance to spend this second life with him.

Nox

As we walked toward the villa, Lionel chattering away at my side, my mind kept turning over all the pieces, trying to figure out what Meredith's next step would be.

There was something, some piece of the puzzle hovering just at the edge of my consciousness. I could almost feel it, the answer on the tip of my tongue, but it was like a layer of mist covered it, keeping it from me.

"I mean, what are the odds a portal even worked inside the Chasm? You surely couldn't have known it would when you went in..." I froze as Lionel's words filtered through my ear, making him jerk to a halt.

"What is it?" Harlan asked, stepping closer to me, his palm falling to my arm and gripping firmly.

"A portal. Fuck, I knew there was something!"

"Uh, care to share with the class?" Lionel asked, and I rubbed my mouth as I started pacing, unable to stay still as my thoughts raced.

"I kept thinking it couldn't be this easy. That a ward, no matter how strong it was, couldn't be the answer we'd been looking for. That there had to be something we were overlooking. Harlan, what if there was a portal inside the Chasm? Would they be able to get out that way?" I demanded, turning to Harlan.

He shook his head, his eyes turning to the Chasm, or the top of the tower that we could see from here. "No matter how much magic they've collected in there, they won't have enough to build a portal strong enough."

"But what if the portal was already there?" I asked, already knowing I was on the right track. Fuck, why hadn't I thought of this before? Had I really been so distracted by having a mate and everything that happened that I'd forgotten something so important?

"Already there? Why would there be a portal in the Burning Chasm?" Harlan asked, clearly confused.

One look at Lionel, and I knew he was on the same track. "The demon realm," he murmured, the realization clear in his voice. "We need to tell Damien."

Quicker than me, he took off, running the few feet left to the villa instead of using his magic to get there. I followed him, Harlan close at my heels. I knew he was confused, but I knew he could wait a few minutes for the answers. Harlan was nothing if not patient. He had to be, to deal with me on a daily basis.

I was so lost in thought I hadn't realized Lionel had stopped until I smacked into his back in the doorway of the lounge, getting a mouthful of white feathers in the process.

Spitting them out, I stepped around him, shooting him a glare. "Why the hell did you stop?"

It was only then that I realized he was rooted to the spot, his eyes wide. "He's my mate," he murmured, a mix of awe and shock in his voice.

"What? Who?" I demanded, glancing into the room, looking for a newcomer that wasn't there. The only person Lionel could possibly be talking about was...no way...

"The king of Afterworld," Lionel murmured.

Well, things just got a whole lot more interesting.

Read the conclusion to this adventure and Lionel and Tharion's story in the next Lords of Otherworld book, <u>Lionel.</u>

Also By Stella

PARANORMAL ROMANCE

Set in Mistvale

Mages of Ravenshire:
Set in the fictional town of Mistvale, Mages of Ravenshire is a series filled with magic, laughs and love. Low on angst and high on sweetness, Mages of Ravenshire will leave you with a smile on your face. Come meet Neya, Pads, April, and all the other fur-babies and their humans, vampires and mages.

Touch of Magic. (Raphael x Jai)

Sleep of Eternity. (Cassian x Gus)

Angel of Death. (Aeron x Niall)

Boxset. (With a special bonus scene.)

Misfits of Mistvale:
With side-characters from Mages of Ravenshire, this series features shifters, half-mermen, werewolves, and many more supernaturals. With the usual dose of fur-babies, found family, and all the Mistvale feels, this series features standalones with a different couple in each book.

Claws. (Devon x Oliver)

Tails. (Jules x Firey)

Bonds. (Joy x Quill x Tate)

Mistvale Spin-Off Novellas:
Featuring various side-characters from the town of Mistvale, these novellas are full of sweet, fluffy romance, and the med-dlesome cast of Mistvale.

My Elf Mate. (Noel x Caleb)

My Dragon Mate. (Raiden x William)

My Elf Daddy. (Daddy/little, Westley x Birch)

My Fae Mate. (Genderfluid MC, Celeste x Hector)

Make A Wish. (Free read, Kezan x Ezra)

Christmas In Mistvale. (Revisit ALL your favorite Mistvale couples and see how they're doing!)

The Mistvale Spin-off Collection (Includes My Elf Mate, My Dragon Mate, My Elf Daddy, and My Fae Mate.)

Mystics of Mistvale:
Featuring some new residents of Mistvale, this series includes a single dad incubus, an elusive griffin, a wise unicorn, a protective gargoyle, and some more unique supes. And of course, you'll revisit some of your beloved Mistvalers from the previous books. With the usual dose of romance, found family, and all the Mistvale feels, this series features standalones with a different couple in each book.

The Elusive Griffin.

Set in Otherworld

Fate's Gambit Trilogy:
Fate's Gambit is an MMM PNR trilogy featuring a sweet, subby cinnamon-bun devil, a gentle-giant who's a service sub/Daddy switch, and a slightly frustrated Master as they slowly figure our their dynamic and fall madly in love. They're joined by annoyingly awesome side-characters including a sweet hedgehog, a sassy talking snake, and a guardian in the form of a cat-man. This trilogy features the same triad: **Damien, Reece, & Artemus**, and needs to be read in order.

First Play. (Free Prequel.)

Devil's Gamble.

Pet's Ploy.

Master's Design.

Boxset.

Lords of Otherworld:
Following the events of Fate's Gambit, Lords of Otherworld delves deeper into the workings of Otherworld, with new characters, new romance, and new adventures. With found family vibes, danger and romance, each book in this series follows a different couple, with an overarching storyline. It is recommended to read the books in order.

Maximus

Zane.

Nox.

Lionel.

Standalones

Elijah Summons A Demon (A newsletter serial.)

CONTEMPORARY ROMANCE

Voice Out

Weathering The Storm (Roommates to lovers, hurt/comfort.)

Watching The Sunrise (Friends to lovers, genderfluid MC.)

Weaving The Stars (Roommates to lovers, age gap, drag performer MC.)

About Stella

Stella Rainbow lives in a small town in India with her family and her five-year-old cat, Harry, who is her number one supporter, cuddle buddy, and writing buddy all rolled into one.

Living with a chronic illness, Stella grew up with books as her best friends, and now she writes in the hopes of giving others like her a reprieve from the real world.

Stella's books are low on the angst, high on the sweetness, with a doze of found family, and some absolutely adorable fur—and sometimes scale—babies.

You can join her mailing list to receive updates about her books and free content. You can also read more about Stella, her books, and the universe she writes in on her website, www.authorstellarainbow.com.

You can also follow her on:

Facebook: Stella Rainbow
Instagram: @authorstellarainbow

Goodreads: <u>Stella Rainbow</u>
BookBub: <u>Stella Rainbow</u>
Amazon: <u>Stella Rainbow</u>